10770647

MASKED & MINE

AN MMF DARK ROMANCE

HIGH STAKES SYNDICATE SERIES
BOOK 0.5

TILLY RIDGE

ISBN: 979-8-218-31590-0

Edit by Sadie at Dot The I Edit

Book Cover & Formatting Images by Disturbed Valkyrie Designs

Formatting by Tilly Ridge

Second edition 2024

DEDICATION

For my fellow unhinged, mask-obsessed whores…

This one's for us.

CONTENT WARNINGS

Masked & Mine is book 0.5 of the High Stakes Syndicate Series. An MMF dark romance with multiple love interests, and the heroine does not pick one hero. The two male love interests already have an established relationship. This book isn't dark in the aspects of killing/murder, but dark in romance aspects. Please know this is an erotic novella, and the plot is merely the background. This was a fun fever dream for me to write, but if you have triggers, please see the link below to my website.

From Chapter sixteen on, is what used to be Forever Masked & Mine. I combined them into the same book to limit confusion. I felt the story wasn't complete until both books had been read.

But again, if you are in need of a plotline… this is not the book for you. No hard feelings, I promise!

<u>Visit tillyridgeauthor.com for a full list of triggers.</u>

PLAYLIST

As you read, you will find footnotes throughout the book—as you will in all of my books. The footnotes will indicate which song is playing at the time of specific scenes. You can play the song until the next footnote indicates a song change or until the chapter ends. The playlist is linked below. I am a big music girly, and it inspires most of my writing. I hope you all enjoy listening as much as you enjoy reading to get the full Tilly Ridge experience!

Numb to the Feeling - Chase Atlantic
Wus Good / Curious - PARTYNEXTDOOR
Say It - Tory Lanez
High For This - Original - The Weeknd
I NEVER EXISTED - Chase Atlantic
DEVILISH - Chase Atlantic

Six Feet Under - The Weeknd
all the good girls go to hell - Billie Eilish
bad decisions - Bad Omens
Porn Star - August Alsina
Pretty Little Fears (feat. J. Cole) - 6LACK, J. Cole
OHMAMI - With Maggie Lindeman - Chase Atlantic,
Maggie LindemanBuy U a Drank (Shawty Snappin') (feat.
Yung Joc) - T-Pain, Yung Joc
STRANGER THINGS - Chase Atlantic
Unholy (feat. Kim Petras) - Sam Smith, Kim Petras
Swervin (feat. 6ix9ine) - A Boogie Wit da Hoodie, 6ix9ine
in these walls (my house) (feat. PVRIS) - Machine Gun
Kelly, PVRIS
Going Bad (feat. Drake) - Meek Mill, Drake
Girls Need Love (with Drake) - Remix - Summer Walker,
Drake
THE DEATH OF PEACE OF MIND - Bad Omens
Dethrone - Bad Omens
Ascensionism - Sleep Token
Never Know - Bad Omens
Into It - Chase Atlantic
You - Jacquees
Unholy - Ana Eclipse
No Need for Introductions, I've Read About Girls Like
You On The Backs of Toilet Doors - Bring Me The
Horizon
Break from Toronto - PARTYNEXTDOOR
Planez - Jeremih, J. Cole
Mask Off - Future
PRETTY WHEN U CRY - PLVTINUM
Right Here - Chase Atlantic
Life is Good (feat. Drake) - Future, Drake
Freek-A-Leek - Petey Pablo
Big Mama - Latto

BEG! - Vana
IF THERE IS A GOD, IT'S ME - PLVTINUM
THE RIDE - Omido, Kae
Backseat - Daniel Di Angelo
SACRILEGIOUS - PLVTINUM
Traphouse - Tory Lanez, Nyce
Recognize (feat. Drake) - PARTYNEXTDOOR, Drake
Another Life - Motionless In White
Take Me to Church - Hozier
ur special to me - Artemas
sun to me - mgk
hell of a good time - Haiden Henderson
Never Lose Me (feat. SZA, Cardi B) - Flo Milli, SZA, Cardi B
ESCORT - Chase Atalntic
Type Shit - Future, Metro Boomin', Travis Scott, Playboi Carti
AMERICAN HORROR SHOW - Snow Wife
Adaptation - The Weeknd

CONTENTS

@KÖNIGOFTHEUNDERWORLD
PERCY

"Come on, Mack, get your shit together." He's getting the cameras set up so we can stream, which should've been done ten minutes ago. We're going to be late for our scheduled time. We always try to jump on around the same time every other evening, but sometimes life gets in the way. Most of the subscribers won't care, but some are beyond unhinged and will be in our inboxes on every platform until they see us on their screen.

"Dude, I'm trying. Chill." As always, he rolls his eyes.

"I'm chill. You know I like having time before having to jump on to settle my nerves. That ass is about to get spanked if those eyes don't quit rolling."

No matter how many times I get in front of this camera, I still get nervous. After a year you would think it would be second nature. We both wear masks the entire time, so that helps comfort me somewhat.

Mack is dressed as Ghost, and I'm dressed in the König get-up, both from the Call of Duty universe. When we met on socials, we found out we both happened to live in

Vegas. Everything came together perfectly—in fact, too perfectly. I keep waiting for the other shoe to drop…

"You ready to get masked up, Schlong Kong?" Mack jokes, like he always does.

Before we started collaborating with each other, we each had a huge fan base, but together we blew the fuck up. Male-on-male content seems to drive people feral for some unknown reason. The strangest part we've come to realize is that it's mainly women viewing our content. But we're not ones to look a gift horse in the mouth.

"Baby, please quit calling me that." He's been calling me "Schlong Kong" for as long as I can remember. The subscribers have picked it up and run with it. He's goofy as fuck, but I couldn't live without this man.

He turns around and shoots a wink. "You love it."

We've officially been dating for eight months now. We both moved out of our apartments and into our perfect little townhome that's about ten minutes off the strip of Vegas. We're far enough away from the chaos, but never too far to use ride share when we're looking to have some fun.

Never in my life did I think I would be a camboy, let alone doing this with another guy, but here I am. Although I have the option, I haven't left my full-time marketing job. My control freak tendencies won't allow it. I enjoy my job as a manager at our company, working directly under the COO, but it's not fulfilling me as much as I had once dreamed. I still have that nagging feeling that I can do better.

"Get out of your head, Percy. I see you spinning out of control. The cameras are ready. Let's get suited up." As soon as we begin the live, Mack usually takes over being his normal, goofy self, and once we get into it, I'll finally crawl out of my anxiety-ridden brain.

Looking into Mack's eyes, I start pulling my shirt over my head with one hand, and he does the same. We're across the room from one another, but the sexual tension is already emanating between us.

Why is pulling a shirt off one-handed so hot?

Mack always looks so good. We always get a workout in before streaming. The little gym is set up in one of our spare rooms, so we don't even have to leave the house if we don't feel like it. The pump is ridiculous for us both, but Mack's veins are out of this world. He has the normal veins littering his arms and tops of his hands, but what has me weak in the knees, are the ones that trail all the way from his pecks down his stomach toward his perfect cock.

We start by pulling our pants on, then strapping each leg up with holsters and, obviously, our masks. While we go all out on TikTok dressing up in our cosplay gear, that isn't the reason we're on this cam site. They want to see it all in the most intimate way—*everything*.

He's buttoning up those black cargo pants, and I'm still over here ogling him. "Do you need help? Fuck, are you already hard?" he questions, tilting his head to the side, staring at me. Palming my cock—goddamn, I am rock hard… All the blood is rushing south from the sight of him trying to get those thick thighs and that juicy ass squeezed into his cargo pants.

I walk over to him, pinning his body against the wall beside the couch. "You know what you do to me, Ghost," I growl beside his ear, rubbing my dick against his.

"I love it when you use my screen name with no cameras going," he huffs. I can already see him, ready to beg. He takes his hands running them down my bare stomach right to my rock-hard cock, palming it. Goose bumps litter my skin from his touch.

"Okay, we have to get on, or you know they're going to

be blowing us up," I say, stepping away from him and quickly putting the rest of my gear on. My headpiece is more like a blanket than a mask, so it's a lot easier to get on than Mack's. I figured it would be more breathable when I started with this cosplay shit, and I was correct. It's the only reason I picked this König character. Mack's is tighter; his entire head and neck are covered in a spandex material, and a hard white material covers his nose and cheeks. My favorite part of his mask is the eye holes that are cut out of the spandex and the piece that sits on top of it.

It's hot as shit.

"I'm so ready to take that perfect, tight ass of yours," I sigh over my shoulder while buckling the black cloth belt around my waist. Hopefully, the subscribers pay up quick so he can get these pants off of me.

He gives me a devious grin, but looks ready to put up a fight, when he says, "What makes you think I'm not taking *your* tight ass tonight?"

"Guess we'll see what the subs want," I counter back while pulling my mask down over my face. Our masks are the only things that stay on our bodies the whole time, without question. I had no clue I had a mask kink until we hung out the first couple of times to collab for socials. But let me just tell you, seeing Mack's glorious body covered in tattoos from head to toe all muscular with those fucking leg holsters.

Yeah, to say I was biting my fist to hold in the noises that were trying to escape me is an understatement.

He happens to be a tattoo artist, and his co-workers persuaded him to get his nipples pierced on a dare. He ended up only piercing his left nipple, and damn it looks so good on him.

Fuck, he looks edible tonight.

[1] I turn our streaming playlist on. He nods his head and hits the button that lets us know we're live. We're sitting on the couch in our living room. We agreed streaming from the living room was best; our bedroom felt a little too personal. Our setup stays in the living room, and explaining the cameras and mic to guests who don't know we do this is always a fun party trick.

We're both lying back, looking at the TV, manspreading to the max, while watching the chats pour in. We can always see at least one of the videos and the chat. It gives the exhibitionist in me a thrill to simultaneously watch what all the subscribers are seeing.

Speaking to the subs, Mack jokes, "Damn, we can't get any foreplay?" And just like that, he's already taking over. It's like he can feel when I'm internally panicking in the beginning. He scoots over toward me on the couch, our legs now touching. "What does everyone want to see tonight? I'm feeling I should be in charge." Fuck, they're going to eat that up. I'm usually the one who takes charge, but I like to call myself a switch. We both do, actually; Mack usually just falls into the more submissive position when it's just us two.

I slide off the couch and onto my knees beside him, announcing, "Good thing I'm always ready to please you, Ghost." I undo his leg holster slowly while he reads off some of the paid chats. Not to brag, but we get so many that we can usually only focus on the paid ones, sadly.

He starts to read them to us:

$87- @GHOSTS_WH0RE

Get Ghost's fat cock out, daddy!

$200- @KÖNIGSMYDADDY

---

1. Numb to the Feeling - Chase Atlantic

> Let Ghost fuck that tight ass, daddy…
> Please.

While looking down at me through his mask, he murmurs, "Oh, look what we have here, König, they want me to fuck that tight hole of yours." I'm fumbling with getting his pants unbuttoned, really not caring what the viewers are saying.

I'm sucking his cock right this moment.

Two cameras are always capturing us when we're filming. One is to the side of us, and the other is directly in front. We can switch them back and forth or do the split-screen version so the viewers can see all the angles. I don't know what angle we're showing currently, and I can't find it in me to care. I just want Mack's dick out and to hear those sweet whimpers falling from his lips.

Helping to pull his pants and briefs down his legs, he kicks them off to spread his legs even wider. I now have such a beautiful view of him as I go back to kneel in front of him. Running my hands up his stomach, I appreciate his abs and the veins that are corded right below his inked skin. I take the bottom of my mask and make sure to tuck it in partially so the subs can only see the lower half of my face. I practically crawl up his upper body and grab his pierced nipple in between my teeth. That has him gasping in shock—probably causing a little pain.

I trail my tongue down his stomach while looking up at him. "Mmm, fill all my holes with this beautiful dick, baby." Those are the last words I get out before he grabs both sides of my head and shoves his cock through my parted lips.

Mack is the definition of a cinnamon roll. This man is covered in tattoos from the bottom of his skull to the smiley face on the bottom of his big toe. He. Is. Absolutely.

Covered. He may look scary as shit, but he's a lover at heart. That is, until you let him take charge in the bedroom.

He bleached his hair recently from its natural chestnut brown. It's grown out a little now, and the platinum shade on top is a perfect complement to his natural color growing in on the sides. He keeps the sides just long enough that you can see the tattoos peeking through the faded hair at the bottom. It's the cherry on top that makes me absolutely feral for this man.

Nights like tonight I forget we're even being filmed, and this site can stream us to over twelve million people. With that thought bouncing around my head, I take him deep to the back of my throat while grabbing his balls. That move causes him to let out a moan, and that's all I need to hear.

Through a clenched jaw, he growls, "Fuck, König, you suck this cock so good." I'm usually the one throwing praises out, but I do love earning some praise myself.

When I slide both hands under his hips and pull him forward, he yelps as his ass hangs off the couch. With his thick cock still stuffed in my mouth, I manage to smile. I put my hand up in front of him, and he knows what I want. I hear him opening the lube bottle, and the cool gel hits my fingers. Still bobbing up and down on his beautiful cock, I take my lubed fingers and press up against his tight hole.

He's practically panting, begging me, "Yesss, please more."

Mocking him, I come off his cock, smirking up at him. "You're already begging, Ghost? I thought you wanted to be in charge tonight?" Slipping one lubed finger in his ass, he's gasping for air even harder. His little noises feed my soul.

Our eyes find one another, as I command him, "Read what the subs are saying, Baby Boy."

H e knows what he's doing by making me read these chats while he has me in his hands like putty on this couch. He's finger-fucking my ass with two fingers—getting me ready for three—rubbing against my prostate. Then add his warm, wet, glorious fucking mouth… yeah I'm heading over the edge embarrassingly quick.

[1] I start to read the chats out loud:

$100- @DUMB_DICK69

> I'd suck that cock any day. Take those clothes off Daddy König. I want to see that pretty hole of yours. 😏

With an audible pop from how hard he was sucking me, Percy releases his hold on my cock then removes his fingers from my ass, leaving me feeling empty. He has been waiting for one of them to tell him to strip, and he finally got that.

---

1. Wus Good / Curious - PARTYNEXTDOOR

It's our way of making easy money. We only do things when our subscribers tell us to. Sucking my cock unprompted was unusual, especially for Percy. He does everything by the book. That's why he's so good at being in charge, and he's sure to top from the bottom when he lets me fuck him.

He takes a step back from me to remove those slutty little holsters that are currently wrapped around his thighs. Then he unbuttons those tight-as-fuck cargo pants. I'm still sprawled out on the couch, my dick lying on my stomach, painfully hard. I openly appreciate him; at six foot four, he's a couple of inches taller than me.

He looks unbelievable with the pump he is currently sporting and the tattoos he let me mark on him. Being able to tattoo that virgin skin awakened the caveman in me that I had no clue was hiding beneath the surface. I've finished his entire chest and both of his sleeves. It's all under-the-sea vibes: squids, wrecked pirate ships, and a couple of wild-looking sharks—but make it spooky. It's still some of my favorite work to this day. Plus, I get to admire it when-ever I want.

I continue to read out loud letting the overhead micro-phone that's screwed into the wall pick up my voice:

$58- @HORSECOCK9000

@Untrained__Ghostt how's that mouth feel?

"His mouth is heaven on Earth." I'm talking to all the subs, but I'm holding eye contact with Percy while he's stripping out of his clothes. His little exhibitionist ass is putting on a show just for me. He couldn't care less about the subscribers or the cameras right now. I haven't seen him this turned on in a while, and the giddiness inside me is growing by the second. He's down to his black briefs that are clinging to his tapered waist, and fuck does he look good. I can see his massive erection positioned down his right thigh, and all I want to do is worship it.

$69- @Y0URBBG!RL

Ghost suck König's cock! NOW!!!

Nope. Not putting up with that.

"Goddamn, you all need to chill out tonight, or we'll end this now." I can physically see Percy's cock twitching from my words.

"Fuck, Ghost, I love it when you talk to the subs that way," Percy practically purrs.

"I can tell, Big Daddy. That cock's doing tricks for me in those briefs." I mock him, making some fake kissing sounds. I love getting under his skin.

He comes barreling at me. I throw my right hand up, stopping him, then ask, "Ah-ah-ah, who's in charge tonight?"

"You," he grinds out like it pains him.

"That's right. Now go lie down on the couch. I have some fun plans for us." He's looking at me like I've officially lost it, but he reluctantly heads over to the couch. And I add to irritate him even more, "And take those damn briefs off already."

He flops down on the couch and looks over at me, waiting to see what I have up my sleeve for us tonight. I slowly walk over and raise his mask so the bottom half is blanketed over the eye holes of his mask. I'm beyond thankful that I get to see the rest of his beautiful face outside of filming… it would be a true disgrace if I couldn't. The man's beautiful.

He can't see a thing, so I take the time to admire his strong jawline that's covered in short, dark hair—how I love a bearded man!

Getting your ass eaten by one is top-tier.

I kneel down and start peppering his jaw and throat with kisses. Eventually, I make my way to one of his tiny pink buds and suck it into my mouth.

"Shit, you shouldn't feel that good, Ghost." He's panting, and we're nowhere near the good part. The buildup is my favorite, but I think that's because I'm a bit of an edger myself. And add it being a man like Percy at my will, begging and pleading to come, is always worth it at the end. Getting him hard and walking away is one of my favorite things—I do that multiple times a day, which gets us to where we are now. I've been teasing this poor man all day long.

Easing up, I look at the TV and see the chat blowing up. Barely above a whisper, I start reading the chat off, directly into his neck. My lips hover right above his skin:

$96- @MASKEDCOCKS

I hope the plan is to 69. If it's not, can it be now?

"Do you hear that, König? Someone wants to see you choking on your Good Boy's cock while I choke on yours. And guess what?" I begin to trail my finger down his tight stomach, over his happy trail, then fisting his thick length in the tight grip that I know he loves. "You're still not going to see a thing, so don't you dare move that mask." His upper body is covered in goosebumps, as he gives me a shiver.

When I want to suck dick, my mask tends to be a lot harder to maneuver. I pull up the mesh cover to free my mouth. Like Percy's, the bottom half of my face is visible. The subs eat this shit up. They love the mystery, but not more than seeing us suck each other off.

Climbing on top of him, I place my knees beside his

shoulders. I drag my cock down his head and move his mask down a little further. He reaches up to help me. "Nope, leave it. Open. Now," I exclaim, removing his hand and shoving my dick into his mouth, which he gladly accepts. I hover above his face so I don't choke him.

At least not yet.

Grabbing his cock with my left hand, I give the head a quick swirl, making sure to collect the drop of pre-cum from the tip. I hum in appreciation as he jumps his hips up, shoving more of him into my mouth.

Tsks. Tsks. Tsks.

"Already topping from the bottom, I see."

I grab the bottle of lube, uncap it, and look at the screen again to see if I need to read more chats.

$64- @GHOSTS__SLUTT

Gag me with that fat cock, please
baby boy.

Damn, some of these comments still shock me.

$37- @CODBOY57

Finger that tight ass of daddy's!! I've been
waiting weeks to see this again!

"Put that mouth back on my cock," Percy barks out. Way too commanding for my liking. Silencing him, I push my cock deep into his throat. I smile, looking directly into the camera as he starts to gag. I lift and lower my hips, sinking deeper and deeper.

"Yeesss, choke on this cock. Fuucckkkk, I love it when—"

Thrust.

"You."

Thrust.

"Gag."

My hands are on his thighs, and I'm hovering over his head to access a better angle into the back of his throat, which gives me the perfect view of the whole scene. A couple more thrusts, and I ease back out so he can have a little more control over how deep he's taking me.

Tapping on his thighs, I utter, "Bend and spread these for me." Grabbing behind his knees, I pull them up even more to the side of his stomach, locking me in place. Fuck, the view from the side camera that's pointed right at us has the perfect shot of his tight little hole.

I grip his ass and pull his cheeks apart, then I announce to everyone, "Look at this tight hole. Oh, you guys must be itching to get your hands on this stunning ass." I can no longer see my cock in Percy's mouth as he starts to wriggle and move his hips from side to side.

Smack!

I bark out, "Hold still! Do you want to be punished?!"

He nods and continues bobbing his head up and down. With the bottle of lube still in hand, I prepare my three fingers. Never knowing how many I'll need to get him prepped.

[2] "Words, König."

"You. You're in charge tonight, babbyyyy." I push my finger into him a lot quicker than I probably should, but am sucking his throbbing cock back into my mouth to ease the sting. Pumping my finger in and out of his ass, I begin to kiss and suck all over his cock. I add another lubed finger and curl them upwards, rubbing back and forth in search of his prostate.

Found it.

Speaking to Percy again, but really taunting the subs, I tease, "Look at you, cock shoved down your throat. Two—

---

2. Say It - Tory Lanez

no, wait"—I push in another finger—"three of my fingers in your ass, and your dick is weeping for me. He tastes delicious by the way." I keep going, looking right into the camera. "Just how I like you. How about you all? Does he look like the best boy right now?" He lets out a low growl, not liking the "best boy" comment. He absolutely hates any kind of praise thrown at him. On the other hand, I eat up the praise given to me.

Pulling out from both his mouth and ass, he lets out the faintest whimper. I move to kneel at the bottom of the couch, giving me the perfect view of him spread out. I lean up, giving him a quick kiss on his swollen lips before I move both our masks back into place.

"How is it being able to see again, König? Read some chats. I want to hear that sultry voice of yours from having my cock in the back of your throat," I whisper just loud enough for the subs to hear. He has the deepest voice I've ever heard in person

$100 - @YOURDADSMYDADDY

Daddy, I love when you're the sub.

$34 - @G0OCHW!ZARD

Ghost, fuck his ass like the good boy you are.

Percy is quick to shut that subscriber down. "You all know better than to call him 'good boy.' That praise is reserved for me, and me only." He is over this shit tonight, and I can tell he's tense. He wants to fuck without the subscribers here and not have to worry about the cameras for once.

I try to take his mind off everything by saying, "I think you're ready for me now, Daddy."

He's still lying back on the couch, as I inch up and

hover over his body. Putting my lips right beside his ear, I whisper, "I need you to let go tonight and trust me. I have you. Okay?"

I pull back to look into his eyes. It's the only thing I can see on his face, but they're saying so much. I see him hand the power over to me, and he nods.

"I love you, Baby Boy." I know he wants to say my real name, but that's a hard line we maintain because fans are absolutely ready to hunt us down and find us in real life.

I pull the bottle of lube back out. You wouldn't believe how much of this we go through, but I mean, try anal without it and report back… That shit isn't fun for either party.

Trust me.

I lather my dick in it and line up with his perfect hole, asking him, "Are you ready? Relax. Let me in."

The littlest whimper comes from Percy, and I'm running with it. "You sound so fucking desperate, Daddy. Whimpering for me to fuck this tight little hole of yours," I growl to him as I push inside inch by inch until my balls are pressed up to the back of him. My self-control is clawing its way out of my body, but I pause, staying buried deep inside him for a second, giving him the time he needs to adjust. I never want to hurt Percy, especially since I'm the only guy he's ever been with.

I tried to stay away from straight guys before I met him, purely because it usually ended with me falling for them, but the feeling was never mutual, or they didn't want to go public. I refuse to hide anything about my sexuality. Meeting Percy, though, that rule went out the window the first time we hung out. I despise the insta-love shit… but I hate to say that perfectly describes us. I just knew—we both did.

We're both bisexual—he's newly awakened—and

sometimes I bring up the topic of women to see where his head is. I've never been one to be on the monogamy train until this last year with Percy, and how could we go wrong to spice things up?

You know what? Let's try it now.

Loud enough for the mic to pick it up, I lazily thrust in and out of him and say, "Could you imagine a woman between us?"

"Where the hell did that come from while you're balls deep in my ass? What am I not enough for you, *baby?*" he practically spits the last word out.

"Damn, for a man who's only had pussy for thirty years, you turn it down quickly. Is this ass that good, Daddy?" Thrusting hard a couple of times, I earn some grunts from Percy. "And this dick is phenomenal, apparently."

The chat is going berserk. I hear the chimes coming in so fast, there's no way we would've been able to keep up with them. Oh well, I'm getting lost in Percy tonight. I do need my answer from him though.

"I love you, König. You know that. You're everything I've ever wanted and dreamed of. But why not branch out and work with a female? Think of all the marketing opportunities." I smirk after saying that one, knowing he can't see my mouth under the mask.

"I know you're not talking about marketing to me while we're fucking." I can hear him smiling through his words. I really wish I could see his perfect teeth beaming at me, but the damn mask is in the way. This is his love language, when I bring up the things he's passionate about.

"You could be fucking her while I'm taking you. We could spit-roast her. Or maybe we can find someone who wants to tell us what to do. Oh, oh, what about one that degrades? I love being degraded." Now he's full-on belly laughing.

Damn, why does that feel so good on my dick?

Once he's done laughing, he answers with a moan, "Yes, we can bring one in, but we must have clear boundaries, and no feelings are to be involved. I refuse to see you hurting. Now please, fuck me, Ghost."

@DEVILS_SOVEREIGN
MARFA

Goddamn, they will not shut the fuck up about these two cosplayers. I close out of my stream and grab the blunt that's been waiting for me on my nightstand all day. I'm trying to relax as my post-orgasm bliss is taking effect after some light degrading work with a couple of my online clients.

My little demons have been hounding me to collaborate with these two guys, but I am not working with another Dom. Don't get me wrong, I eat up the thought of being with two guys and also getting to see them fuck each other. But I would need full control over both of them, and since one of them is used to being in charge, I don't see how this could work.

After seeing what seems like the twenty-first comment and tag asking when our collaboration will happen, I finally cave and log onto the cosplayer's stream. The subs know I'm in Vegas because I used to talk about working at Sins. Guess where the cosplayers live… *Vegas*.

This year, the masked men craze on social media really took off. I'm guessing these two ran with it. They're newer to the cam world, like me, but clearly, they've got this shit figured out. Who doesn't love a man in a mask? Hot as fuck men at that. Here I am, drooling over their muscular, tattooed bodies, even though their builds are vastly different.

König is a little taller and leaner, but his chest is wide, and his arms are incredibly muscular. His waist tapers down with the finest V-cut I've ever seen, and his thighs look like they could crush things for fun. Ghost is what I think of when I hear the word "meathead." He's still tall enough to tower over me, but his arms look like I could dangle from them like gymnasts do on the bars.

I jump onto their live stream to see what all this hype is about. The first thing I see is König getting fucked in the ass.

Wait… What?

I thought he was the dominant top? Maybe I have their whole dynamic wrong? Both switches? If that's the case, I'll gladly be in charge of both of them.

[1] How this is my life right now, I'll never know. Watching these two random guys fuck on my laptop, I decide to shoot my shot on this live chat. I type into the chat:

@DEVILS_SOVEREIGN

I have been summoned here.

My heart rate is picking up, and I have no clue why. I shouldn't be nervous around them. I've done this before, just not with two hot-ass men, at the same time.

That also fuck each other.

The guy-on-guy makes it even more enticing, but also… tag me in, coach.

---

1. High For This - Original - The Weeknd

I'll peg a man any day.

I will more than happily be in the middle of these two. The chats are flying in. My eyes practically bug out of my head. They want this bad.

$30- @KÖNIGGS_COCKGOBBLER

@Devils_sovereign has arrived!!!!

$50- @DADDYS_D!RTYWH0RE

@Devils_sovereign domme them both, PLEASE!!

$16- @YOURGOODBOY

@Devils_sovereign can run me over.

$100- @ILLPAYYOURBILLS

I'll pay whatever to get all three of them in front of the same camera.

Damn, hopefully they'll pay some of my bills too…

I recognize some names from my chat. I'm guessing they've made their way over here. Ghost and König aren't even paying attention to the chats; you can tell they are so into each other. The chemistry is off the charts, and I can't even see their faces. The cameras are just there, and here we are, lucky enough to watch.

"Yessss, come for me, Daddy. You better not touch that fat cock of yours. I want you coming just from my dick in your ass. Milking that prostate." Calling him Daddy while he's fucking him isn't something I thought my cunt would react to… but here we are.

She's reacting.

Ghost is pounding into his ass so hard, enunciating each word while handing out punishing thrusts. He has König's legs bent up into his armpits which puts Konig's ass on Ghost's thighs. Honestly, it's the perfect angle to get to his prostate; it makes me wonder if he knows his way around a woman's anatomy, too.

I'm not paying attention to anything besides them. The chemistry between these two is palpable. I've always been a voyeur, but this takes it to another level.

König grunts out, "I'm coming, Baby Boy! Fuck, Ghost, yes!" Cum is pouring out of his cock. I'm fascinated. He's not even touching his dick. I've seen nothing like it, and I watch with rapt attention as it keeps going and going. I'll be storing that little tidbit of info away for later… It's pooling on the base of his cock, balls, and stomach. And I'd happily clean him up.

What the fuck is happening to me?

It's the masks. That's what I keep telling myself. I'd pay a pretty penny to get in between these two. Now I see why so many obsessed subscribers spend tons of money on them. I shouldn't have been so annoyed with them. This could change my life—for my cam business, that is. Hell, I'd take them allowing me to sit and watch while I take charge, giving both of them orders to do all kinds of filthy shit to each other without me even touching them. I don't know if they're in an open relationship or just film with each other for business. If the subscribers are adamant about collaborating, they must have discussed the idea at some point.

Setting my blunt between my lips, lighting it. I inhale, holding it in for a few seconds, releasing the smoke, laying my head back on my pillow, and finally relaxing. I don't like to be out of my mind high, but high enough to make everything feel good.

Especially orgasms.

As I watch the guys, my other hand drifts down my stomach. I'm still naked from being online earlier, and in my position, slumped back on my bed with my laptop beside me, it wouldn't hurt to rub another one out real quick, right?

I dip two fingers down into my wetness, coming back up to rub big, slow circles over my already swollen clit.

"Please. Please. Please," König begs.

"Please what?" Ghost asks.

"I want your cum, baby. Please, in my ass." Fuck, seeing König beg, knowing he's usually in charge, has my pussy throbbing.

"I'm not your baby right now, König." Bless the fucking Devil for a switch that can really switch.

"Fuck! Ghost, please! Please, use me like your little fuckdoll… Just for tonight." He begs so pretty.

"You better hold on." It's the last thing Ghost grunts out before he hammers deeper into König's ass. König has already come, but his erection never went away. Ghost runs his hand through König's cum, fists his cock, and starts pumping his hand up and down at the same punishing pace that he's pounding into him. The grunts coming from Ghost and the whimpers coming from König have me rubbing my clit with sure pressure. I don't have it in me to be a switch and give all the props to them.

But I sure as hell love to watch one.

My hand is moving side to side, as if I'm right there with them. I know the chat's probably going wild. How could anyone type instead of focusing on what's happening on their screen?

I can feel my orgasm building as I rock my hips up and down, desperately craving more friction. Most of the time, I use one of my many toys, but something hits different when you get it done the old-fashioned way.

The whimpers, begging, and grunts send me spiraling into oblivion. I need this played on repeat.

"Come for me again, König," Ghost growls, but I can

hear the submissive tone wanting to claw its way out of him.

I come as they do. Already feeling some weird connection with these two guys that I can't even explain—yet to see their faces.

Certifiable, right?

My eyes are closed, and my head is thrown back in bliss, but I can still hear them. My orgasm is finally letting up after what feels like forever. I open my eyes again to see them going through the chats, reading some out loud in their post-orgasm bliss. They're still a ways up from where I came in, so it'll be a minute. "Daddy" is sitting sprawled out on the couch beside Ghost. He lifts the bottom part of both their masks and lays the sweetest kiss on Ghost's lips. He whispers something to him that I can't hear. I don't know how I feel about the "Daddy" shit, but working at Sins opened my mind to a lot.

I really can't believe this is what my life has come to. No one, and I mean no one, trusts me in this stupid fucking town. I am fortunate enough to have a piece-of-shit father, Igor Abdulov, who runs the Russian Bravata here in Vegas.

And not well, I must add.

Marfa Sovereign.

That's the last name I chose to get further from under my father's thumb. He obviously didn't take that well. You know, disgracing the Abdulov name and all. I chose Sovereign just to piss him off even more. He's the one who trained me to play the mind games, but that's neither here nor there.

Growing up in his house for eighteen years was enough for me. It's left me in a shit position. I just lost my favorite job I've ever had at the sex club, Sins, as a VIP server. Right before I got let go, a client of the club told me to start this cam-girl gig. He knew I was a dominant woman after I broke a man's arm for touching another server, and told me people would pay a pretty penny to be degraded or even humiliated like that man was.

And here I am, watching these two random men read through chats.

Their wild fan base is exactly what I need, though… I committed a long time ago not to take any more money from my father or the crime organization he runs. I can't say the same about my other parent, if I can even call her that. Tori, my cunty mother, ran off when I was about ten. She didn't go far; she still lives in the city, but was never around or reached out to me when I was growing up.

As soon as I was old enough to work, I got my first job as a waitress at a diner. I did it mainly to get out of my father's house and to start saving up as much money as I could to move out. Once I had enough saved, I got myself a little apartment after I turned eighteen, and I haven't looked back since. Igor didn't like me moving out and being unprotected, but here I am, still living on my own three years later.

I'm finally twenty-one, which has opened up a lot of doors to bartend at some local bars and eventually landed me my dream job at Sins, but that quickly turned to shit. I'm not dumb enough to think Igor doesn't keep tabs on me, but for now, he lets me be. I still need to figure out why Vincent, the owner of Sins, wanted me gone, but right now I'm going to focus on König reading the live chat.

"What do we have here?" Ghost calls out. Fuck, I think they're at my chat.

He's pulling his phone out.

Am I breathing?

My phone vibrates beside me.

No, I'm not breathing…

What. The. Fuck.

I have a direct message from an @Untrained__Ghostt.

@UNTRAINED__GHOSTT

The subscribers clearly love you.

I look back up at the screen, and he's pulled his mask up halfway and is looking directly into the camera, his grin stretching from ear to ear. This fucker thinks he's slick, and he clearly knows I just watched the two of them.

@DEVILS_SOVEREIGN

I just watched that performance. 7/10. I think I could spice things up for the both of you. If you're into women, and open to sharing.

Wipe that smile off your face, too.

Feeling real bold aren't you, bitch? And 7/10? You just came harder than you have in a while. Hilarious, Mar.

@UNTRAINED__GHOSTT

7/10?!!! Who are you kidding? You clearly liked something if you stuck around for so long.

Can we tell Percy 10/10 so I can top again?

Also, I'm Mack. My partner is Percy, ob-vi. Lets meet up. You sound fun, and not to mention you're drop dead gorgeous.

We're both bi. BTW.

Does that bio say Domme? I need nothing else.

Okay, I probably scared you away, sorry about the rambling, and the six messages lol.

He is rambling, but I was so invested in the incoming messages that I hadn't even noticed they ended the stream.

@DEVILS_SOVEREIGN

Yes, you read that right. Miss domme here, not for free though. 😏

I'm down. When do you want to meet?

@UNTRAINED_GHOSTT

Tomorrow, our place?

Tomorrow, is he high?! I act like I have anything else to do. Tomorrow is a Saturday, too. I normally would've been working; it was usually one of our busiest days at the club… Guess that doesn't matter now.

@DEVILS_SOVEREIGN

Okay, I'm down. Send me the address. Is this how the girls are lured to a serial killer's house? Probably.

Good thing I'm not the whimpering damsel in distress.

* * *

[2] I'm chanting "Please don't be ugly, please don't be ugly" while I'm walking up Percy and Mack's driveway. Masked men usually aren't the easiest on the eyes, from experience. But that's the fantasy, right?

It feels weird not to call them König and Ghost. I was really surprised when Mack opened up and told me their names right away. I'm probably looking into it too much. They probably do this with every girl they lure into their house.

---

2. I NEVER EXISTED - Chase Atlantic

Meeting them for the first time at their house probably isn't the best decision on my part. What if they really are killers?

Bitch, you act like your father's not a killer.

What a way to go, though. Two masked men taking me out.

I walk up the steps to the cutest little townhome I've ever seen and knock on the door. A brief moment passes, and the door opens as I look up to see who opened the door. Goddamn, why is this man so tall? It's König—I mean Percy. The definition of tall, dark, and drop-dead fucking gorgeous.

My gut feeling was right… He's so pretty.

Why this man covers his perfect face with a damn mask beats me. He has eyes that take your breath away; they are the lightest blue I have ever seen with little white flecks spread throughout. It's such a stark difference to his pitch-black hair and olive skin shade. He has a beard, but it's trimmed.

Hopefully, I'll be taking that for a test drive.

"Marfa? I'm Percy. So nice to finally meet you in person."

"Aren't you proper? Call me Mar. Honestly, I'll take whore over Marfa." He throws his head back, laughing. I didn't think that was that funny, but I let him have his laugh.

Hands wrap around Percy's waist from behind. "Hi, Mar! I feel like we're already besties. Come on in. I'm obviously Mack."

Peeling off the back of Percy, he walks through their entryway. Mack is a fine specimen, that's for sure. A little bit shorter than Percy, but definitely more built. That's saying a lot because Percy's built like a brick shithouse.

Both of their eyes are piercing, but in different ways.

Mack's are green, but it's such a bright shade of green that's brought out even more by his hair. It's bleached out on the top, but the sides are a natural dark brown color that's shaved toward his scalp. Damn, I wonder who does his hair; it looks good. And compared to Percy's skin, Mack's is a lighter, creamier shade. He's just… pretty. It's almost scary. It makes me want to sit in front of him with my phone and snap pictures of him twenty-four seven.

Percy waves his hand out in front of him, gesturing for me to come in. Wow, he really is so proper… I guess I wouldn't even say he's proper, but he does look more uptight.

I don't know how any of this is going to work…

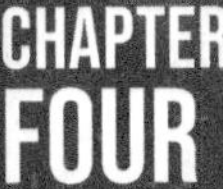

CHAPTER
FOUR

@KÖNIGOFTHEUNDERWORLD
PERCY

Wow, she's beautiful beyond words. Her hair is almost completely black but it has an underlying warmth to it. [1] Her curls are unruly and natural. Those luscious, fuckable lips have a softness that I'd love to feel all over my body. High cheekbones accentuate her brown eyes that feel like they're looking deep into my soul—deeper than they should for meeting only seconds ago. But I guess she did see me get fucked last night, so there's that. Her black-winged eyeliner accentuates her slightly-tilted almond eyes, and I can't stop looking at them. Her amber skin almost appears to be glowing.

She's captivating.

Mack said she's a Domme. He then had to tell me what the hell that term meant because I was obviously clueless. I blame that on my old age. Apparently, it means that she's a female Dom, which makes sense because she screams "I'll gladly stomp on your balls with a stiletto."

Actually, make that platformed boots, not stilettos.

---

1. DEVILISH - Chase Atlantic

"Quit ogling her, goddamn. You're going to scare her off," Mack half-heartedly jokes, slapping my chest.

Mack and I go to sit on the couch side by side, throwing my arm over the back of the couch behind him. Mar sits beside us on one of our emerald velvet chairs. Her legs are crossed, and she's staring at us unconcerned by the fact that we're arguing like the old married couple I wish we were.

"She's breathtaking. How am I not supposed to gawk?" I question him.

She really is.

The way the early afternoon light hits her through the double windows is making her brown eyes glow, accentuating a beautiful reddish tint within them. The short, high-waisted black leather skirt she has on has her thick thighs spilling over the edges. Hitting her beautiful curves just right. The cropped Bad Omens shirt—which she got automatic bonus points for when I opened the front door—barely conceals her killer tits.

She's either got a damn good poker face or she's not fazed by the compliments or our antics, at all. I hate to say it, but most people fall at our feet. We're constantly getting the most unhinged comments on our social media.

"On my knees for you."

"Until my jaw locks."

"That mask looks like the perfect seat."

"There's a tear running down my leg, Daddy."

You name it, it's in our comment section. It's a breath of fresh air that she's not fangirling over us, if I'm honest.

Clapping her hands together—scaring the shit out of me—she questions, "Are you all ready to talk business?"

"Damn, straight to the point." Mack chuckles.

I tilt my head to the side. "What were you wanting to chat about?"

"The collab that all the devils, and whatever the hell you call your subscribers, are foaming at the mouth for." The devils—that's cute as fuck. She wears these little red glowing Devil horns when she streams, per the pictures plastered everywhere. It's all very on-brand for her—making the marketing manager in me so fucking hard.

I start to explain our situation. "Since you brought it up, we have considered sharing a woman. Mack mentioned the idea last night on camera, and the subscribers were freaking out over the possibility of us bringing someone else in." We didn't even have any idea of who that would be, but the subscribers definitely had recommendations—the main one being Mar.

It's only ever been Mack and me, but I think this whole collaboration will be great for business. Before Mack, I thought I was straight; after meeting him, it became obvious that I was bi-curious. We became friends, and he never made a move because he thought I was only into women. One night, I got on my knees for him and haven't looked back since. He's twenty-four, but he's been openly bisexual since he was in high school, and I envy him for it. I was already thirty when we met, and I feel like an old man around him most days.

"We're really only wanting to share one woman, so it doesn't get messy. You know, with testing and safe sex strictly for business. Hopefully, that will send traffic to your page, and we can do collabs whenever. Then we can have the best of both worlds."

"So you're willing to give up power and control? That's one thing I will not do—give up my control," she says as her brows pull together.

I'm confused, that's all she responds with? But answer her truthfully, "I'm going to see how I react to it. I've given up control with Mack plenty of times, but I never go fully into that subspace, and I want to experience that. Having such a tight grip on everything in my life, I want someone to help me let go of that control fully. I need to test those limits more, but most of the time, Mack doesn't like to go full Dom," I give Mack a small hand squeeze. His dominant side comes out occasionally, but not as much as I need. We've communicated about it multiple times, but I never want to push or make him uncomfortable.

"We can test your limits and see what you enjoy," she says with a wild smirk on her face. "I have an IUD, and I haven't been with anyone in a little over a year. I've been tested since then, so we should be safe." She shrugs. Continuing on, she says, "I don't want you all calling me by my name on stream. I have some fans who know me from Sins, but most don't know my actual name. I really don't like the idea of them knowing I live here, but what can you do?" She shrugs again like it's no big deal, but I can tell it's something she's very serious about. "I need full control over both of you while streaming, too."

I wince internally—knowing damn well she's dominant. But it still worries me to fully give her my trust after only just meeting today.

I have to nudge Mack; his jaw is slack, mouth hanging open while he asks, "Over a year?! How the hell?"

Leave it to Mack to ask questions that don't need to be asked.

"I'm very particular, and honestly, my toys can do a better job than most men. I don't like the jealousy that comes out of relationships, and working at the club is hard for some men to accept. Their egos can't handle it." She finger-quotes around "egos," and continues, "I've found that no one can keep the jealousy at bay with a girlfriend who works at a sex club, so I mostly just keep to myself."

"So, you do want to keep things casual?" I ask with rapt curiosity.

She doesn't even hesitate before answering, "Yes, I think casual would be best. I don't catch feelings easily, and I definitely don't want to come between your relationship."

She's going to be shaken to her core when she's between us. It pisses me off that she's only been with dumbass men who can't please her properly. Mack was an excellent teacher when I started exploring with him, so I'm vowing to teach him everything I know to make a woman feel good. He hasn't been with many women, as he always leaned more toward men, but he still had an attraction to some women, not shy to appreciate them.

Now, all that's playing in my mind is both of us on our knees for her.

Fuck, this is not the time to be getting hard right now.

Changing the subject, I reply, "Well, do you only do the cam sites?"

She's shaking her head. "No, I have everything spread out, trying to find which I like the best."

In my opinion, the best part is the interaction with our subscribers. Although our cam clients are our highest-paying customers, they also make the most outrageous requests. Although, it's truly mindless work since I'm a marketing expert. While we both make enough money to quit our full-time jobs, we're currently trying to pay off our little townhouse.

Mack pulls me out of my thoughts, replying, "Not saying we want to bring you into our relationship, but none of us can get jealous if we want this to work." She nods at that, and he throws her question back at her. "What about you? Why do you want to do this?"

"Clearly, you have a loyal fan base. I've been wanting to find higher-paying clients who want to be degraded privately or more subscribers in general. I need to grow on all of my platforms. Degrading is by far my favorite kink, and I just got fired from Sins: In Sin City, the sex club on the strip. So, I'm doing this full time now." She says that last part like she is ashamed—that's the first time I've seen vulnerable emotion from her. "What about you, Mack? What's in this for you?"

I'm curious about his answer, too.

"Look, I don't want this to be taken the wrong way; I love Percy—I always will—but he has mainly slept with women. I've also never really been one to fall into the monogamy norms, necessarily, and that's what we have in this relationship. I'm not saying anything is wrong with it, but with us both being bisexual, I feel like we could get the best of both worlds by doing this. Why should we put ourselves in a box based on societal norms when we don't have to?" Damn, that was a good answer.

She's so intrigued by what Mack has to say—probably from him not being the biggest fan of monogamy, which tends to throw people for a loop. "I get that. It's always fun to explore, as long as everyone is down with it," she replies with a devilish grin.

"Mack has opened my eyes to a lot of shit, clearly. Cue the bi-awakening that happened to me almost a year ago when we first met." I look over at Mack, giving him a smile. God, I love this man. Let's hope this doesn't scare him off. "I'm going to share a deep, dark fantasy with you both, but you have to promise not to judge. I don't think Mack even knows about it, but you'll need his help to make it come to life. It's also my next huge marketing scheme."

I'm hoping like hell they don't judge me for it. It's definitely known as a common thing to fantasize about, but most people obviously don't act on it. And my certifiable ass wants to film it, as well as make it a pay-per-view event

—mainly to be an option for people to live out their fantasies through us. They both give stern nods when my eyes meet each of theirs.

Well, here goes nothing. "I want to be drugged, kidnapped, and fucked… and I want you to film it because it's going to be our next big thing." I don't add in the part where I want to watch it back myself whenever I want.

I expect gasps and shock from both of them, but Mar has that devilish smirk on her face, clearly plotting something.

Mack laughs almost uncontrollably before finally getting out. "Who knew all I needed to do was hit up a Domme to bring out your wild side?"

* * *

[2] I set up the camera to shoot the marketing pictures for our collaboration announcements on all our social media. Later, we'll have to take some semi-PG ones in full gear.

We've been chatting and eating takeout for the last couple of hours; Mack and Mar are in the kitchen, cleaning up quickly while I change into my gear and get everything ready.

Mar is great to be around. She's honestly effortless, which is not usually how women in my past were. We plan to post these pictures tomorrow and cam together for the first time sometime next week. I think I overheard Mack and Mar saying something about wanting to go out tonight. Something about shaking some ass?

"Mack, Mar, come on. Let's get this done," I yell, trying to get their asses to hurry the hell up.

Mack comes walking in with his full gear on, but his

---

2. Six Feet Under - The Weeknd

mask is still off. He immediately drops to the floor and starts doing push-ups. I roll my eyes, but I start doing the same thing. The pump is necessary for good pictures.

I hear Mar walking in when the footsteps stop suddenly, and she questions, "What the hell are you two doing?"

Mack retorts, "Getting a pump on, sweet cheeks."

Before I can blink, Mar is standing between our heads, her boot stepping on Mack's fingers. Luckily, it's his left hand. The right hand is his moneymaker with his tattoo machine.

Mack gasps in shock, and Mar seethes, "It's Sovereign, or Ma'am, to you when we're streaming, and no stupid-ass pet names for me. Ever."

"Okay, okay. I'm sorry, Ma'am," Mack's apologizing profusely, and I'm trying not to laugh at him.

Dropping down onto my stomach, I ask, "Where the hell did you even get sweet cheeks from?" She finally lifts her boot off his hand.

Mack moves to sit on his knees while looking up at her. "Those sweet ass cheeks, that's where. You're a goddess, Ma'am. Sovereign doesn't explain you well enough. You're a god."

She squats down by his face and seethes while tapping his cheek a couple of times. "No, the Devil, babe."

I snap a couple of pictures of them like this. Mack is on his knees, looking up at our real-life Devil. She brought her little glowing-red horns with her; I guess she keeps them in her bag.

She looks so powerful—like she belongs in charge. Now I'm wondering what happened in her life that made her need to be in control and have power over situations. I have to tell myself not to get into these types of thoughts. I'll end up getting attached, and she doesn't seem like the one you get to keep. I mentally note that I will protect Mack and his heart. He'll for sure fall for her, no questions asked.

If he hasn't already.

While looking me in the eyes, she says, "I want you both on your knees for my promo picture." She then casts her eyes down to the floor beside Mack, making her demand clear. My naturally more dominant nature has me wanting to disobey, but I also don't want to be bratty. I guess she thinks we're using separate pictures for our promos.

We aren't.

These are going to be hot as fuck.

I get to my knees and look up, waiting for her next command. I hand the remote that controls the camera over to her while making sure we're all in frame. She grabs our masks, hands them over, and we throw them on. She's in between us, reaching both of her hands down and tilting our chins up to look at her. I hear the *click* of the camera.

She moves her hands to the back of our heads. *Click.*

Then starts to push our heads together. *Click.*

Mar reaches down and lifts both of our masks up with one finger. *Click.*

Then the commands start coming again, "Hover over each other's lips, but don't kiss just yet." Fuck, this is so hot. I'm already getting a chub. *Click.*

"Touch each other, but only one hand each." I go for Mack's hip, and he lands on my bicep that's closest to the camera. *Click.*

"Now, unbuckle your belts." We start fumbling to unbuckle our belts as fast as possible. I didn't think anything was going to happen tonight, but the sexual tension that is flowing between all of us is unbearable. Our belts hang open. *Click.*

I set the camera up facing our normal streaming spot. Then I ask the question that's been bouncing around in my head since we started taking these pictures, "Should we stream but have you off camera telling us what to do as a little teaser to our cam subscribers?" I send prayers down to the Devil that she says yes—this will be great practice for me.

With raised brows, she asks, "Are you two going to be good boys and listen to what I say?"

I'm internally cringing. I hate being called a good boy, but I can tell that Mack is eating out of the palm of her hand already. He's nodding like a goddamn bobblehead, and I find myself nodding along too.

Fuck it, I want to see what all this hype around her is.

CHAPTER FIVE

@DEVILS_SOVEREIGN
MARFA

"Good," I respond while smirking at both of them.

They're getting all the cameras set up and ready to go live. They have a fancy-ass setup, and I am sitting here wondering if I need to get some recommendations from them because my setup looks amateur compared to theirs.

Mack is looking at me like a kid in a candy shop. He's practically skipping at this point, ready to get this show on the road.

"Okay, are you ready?" Percy asks, looking at me.

"Yes. Both of you get on your knees in front of the couch and look up at the camera."

[1] Their pants are slung so low on their hips, and with their eyes on me, they look completely disheveled. Both of their dicks are straining against their pants. I groan internally, they look fucking ediable. "My needy little masked sluts. Look at both of you, patiently waiting for my orders."

---

1. all the good girls go to hell - Billie Eilish

I can feel Percy trying to hold back. We'll work on finding his limit, even if he hasn't fought me on anything so far.

I walk over to the computer, making sure I'm out of view on both cameras.

Yeah, both cameras. I wasn't kidding about their setup.

I hit the live stream button. What makes it even hotter is that they have the live stream up on the TV in the living room, so I feel like I'm watching it twice—live and on the big screen.

We're playing the waiting game until their subscribers start flowing in. I walk back over to the velvet accent chair and take a seat beside the side-view camera. Let me tell you, I have never been more excited not to be wearing underwear under this leather skirt. My eyes just about bug out of my head when I see how many subscribers are already on. They will be eating out of the palm of my hand by the end of this.

Luckily, I'm close enough to the mic that hangs over the couch.

This side-view camera is almost reaching over my shoulder with its tripod, so it works out perfectly for what I have planned. With my sternest voice, I begin talking to the subscribers, "We have new rules tonight. I'm in charge from here on out. Not any of you, and definitely not König or Ghost."

The chats are flowing in at a sick pace already:

$27- @GHOSTSCUMSLUT

Is that @Devils_sovereign? Please be THE SOVEREIGN!!!!

$100- BITCHTHATISMASKED

Get in between them now, ma'am!!! God, I'm so thankful I got on tonight!

$40- @MA$KEDWH0RE

Sovereign, you're living everyone's dream
right now!

I bark out, "If I see God being thanked during the rest of this stream, I won't get these two whores to read any of your worthless chats for the rest of this stream."

Mack and Percy are just staring at me, heads cranked to the side. Oh, I wish I could see their mouths; I bet they're wide open.

I should've brought my harness and cock to shove in their mouths.

I give quick instructions to Percy, "Read a couple of chats, König,"

$75- @KÖNIGISDADDY

I just want to be good for mommy, daddy.

Eh, I kinda like the "mommy" and the way he just moaned it. König keeps on reading:

$16- @MASK&BOOKEDDOWN

I bet Ghost is eating this up, rn.

"Now that you say that, Ghost has been a very good boy today… He is the reason all this started—by reaching out to me and setting up today's meeting. Why don't you get your hard cock out for your boyfriend, Ghost? Then stand up and turn to face me. I want to watch those pretty eyes of yours roll to the back of your head."

He turns around and drops his pants in the same turn. Wow, I have to mentally tell myself to keep it together. I know he's got a smug look on his face under that damn skull mask. If only I could see it…

His body is a true work of art. He's the perfect height, which is about a foot taller than my five-foot-two self. He's covered—I mean, *covered*—in tattoos from head to toe. He literally showed me the smiley face that's on the bottom of his goddamn big toe. I had to tell him I didn't have a foot fetish. I was worried for a second about where he was going with that conversation. Pair all that with the mask—I almost bite my fist to hide a groan.

Percy is still on his knees, facing the TV, making sure to really listen to my commands.

He can be a good boy, after all.

[2] "König, are you ready to play, Big Daddy?" I call out to him. I think I hear the smallest of grunts. Oh, he likes that one. I know he loves the "Daddy" shit, but the "big" added onto it makes it just condescending enough not to make my skin crawl.

Maybe I'll pull out "Papochka," so it's slightly different.

"Suck Ghost's cock better than you ever have, and I might bring that dark fantasy of yours alive tonight." He whips his head around toward me so fast. I think I see excitement in his eyes, and he proves me right at the speed he's crawling over to Mack's eagerly awaiting cock.

He reaches up for Mack's cock when I stop him. "Ah, ah. Stand up and strip, König. I want that pretty asshole winking at me while you're sucking him off."

I've let the chat slip out of my mind until the sounds of them constantly coming in remind me to read some off while I try not to drool over Percy's body. He's a couple of inches taller than Mack, but Mack has more muscle on him. Percy has that slutty little waist I can't wait to strad-dle. I'm making a mental note to get him a crop top. His tattoos are more concentrated—two full sleeves that fully connect over his chest. They seem to tell a story when you look at them, and after Mack told me all about tattooing him earlier, it all started to make sense.

---

2. bad decisions - Bad Omens

Answering the subscriber, I reply, "Not tonight; you're just getting a sneak peek into the fun of what's to come."

Who wouldn't go to fucking Paris with these two?
And we don't mean the city.
"Yes, I'll be getting spit-roasted. Fuck you very much," I chuckle as I answer, and so does Mack.

Mack is looking down at Percy, but I want all the attention right now. I lift my oversized T-shirt over my head and throw it at Percy. They both look over at me, and it's silent. I didn't have a bra on either, so my tits are on full display. Taking both of my legs, I prop my feet up on the edge of the chair and drop my knees to the armrest. My bare pussy out, my skirt pulled up over my legs, and no underwear covering me.

I don't even think they're breathing.

I question, "Ghost, *Luchik*, are you okay? You're awfully quiet."

By boomer beauty standards, I should be self-conscious of my body the way it is. Their silence would stress most women out, thinking they're both picking apart my body. I truly don't think they are. I'm not a size four. Not even in my wildest dreams. I'm curvy—plus size, to be exact. I have stomach rolls, stretch marks, and non-perky tits, but guess what? People love different shit, and it doesn't make me less than someone living in a smaller body than me. The motto I've lived by has always been, "You don't like it, don't look."

König breaks the silence first. "Ma'am… You can't tease us with that beautiful pussy. Please. I'm already on my knees. What else do we have to do?"

Purring, I say, "I love hearing you beg, König. Now suck his cock. Show me what you got, and maybe we can play after."

"Fuck, Sovereign, you're perfect." Mack's voice is dripping with sex.

I'm smirking. "Thank you, *Luchik;* so are you. Now get that pretty dick of yours into your drool-worthy boyfriend's mouth before I combust."

He takes his cock in his hand, moving Percy's mask over his eyes so he can get to his mouth.

"Open your mouth, Daddy," he says while rubbing the tip along the seam of Percy's lips. "Are you going to let me fuck this throat while I watch Sovereign play with that pretty pussy of hers? I bet you all wish you had my view right now." He's throwing that last little bit for the viewers.

Oh, how I love a golden retriever man with a filthy mouth.

Putting two of my fingers into my mouth, sucking them nice and slow, only to tease the hell out of Mack. He drops his head slightly, his eyes still on me through the holes in his mask.

Pulling off Mack's dick, Percy's back to begging, "Please join us, Mama." He's hanging onto every word.

In a threatening tone, I reply, "You beg like a filthy slut, König. I know you heard me earlier. Suck him better than you ever have, and we'll play after the stream. Ghost, you're the judge of whether it's good or not. No acting to boost Big Daddy's ego, either."

There's so much more interaction on their page, it's almost hard to believe. I might as well read some chats before it gets too hot and heavy.

$20- @PRA!SE$LUT99

This is the hottest thing I've ever witnessed.

"Of course it is, babe. Have you seen these two?" I laugh while speaking to the subscriber. Percy and Mack hardly ever comment back to them, but I do. I love starting some shit and egging people on. Honestly, I'm surprised Percy hasn't thought of that. It's bound to make them even more money by getting the crowd all worked up.

Grabbing Mack's balls and taking him to the back of his throat, Percy is putting in some work on Mack right now. The gagging is doing something to my insides. I really fucked myself by not joining in on this, but I do have a front-row seat. Plus I'm in charge, so I can't complain too much. Mack hasn't taken his eyes off me this whole time.

$200- @GHOSTCANTRAINME

Please, get them to sixty-nine again. I'll pay anything!!

Announcing to Percy and the subscribers, I reply, "König is learning to take orders like a good boy, so he's going to stay on his knees pleasing Ghost for tonight. I wouldn't waste any more money trying to get König's happy ending. Ghost gets what he wants." I smirk at Mack while throwing fake kisses at him. He's not used to this treatment, and I don't think he knows quite how to handle it. A flustered man is one of my favorite things...

"The only thing I want tonight is for you to be spread out and devoured by both of us," Mack exclaims with heat in his voice.

"You have your hot-ass boyfriend on his knees with your cock down his throat... Do you hear those sounds? He loves sucking you, *Luchik*." Fuck, I wish I could see his whole face right now. That nickname practically fell out of me earlier, but it felt right.

"Fuck, König." He has both hands on the sides of his head now and is gearing up to start the face fuck of a lifetime.

"I want that throat sore," I declare to both of them. Mack's picking up speed now. "That's right, fuck his throat. Use him for your pleasure, Ghost."

The gagging sounds leaving Percy have me sucking my fingers again and moving them down toward my dripping pussy. I want this as a saved audio. The gagging and whimpering are one thing, but the fact that it's Percy making the noises is even better.

Whimpering men, yes. Yes, that's all I have to say.

Rubbing my clit in tight circles and leaning my head back on the chair just listening, I snap my head back up when I hear Mack grunt, "I'm about to come."

I bark out, "Stop!" Percy stops mid-suck. Damn, he can take my orders so well. "I want your cum tonight." I'm looking Mack right in the eyes.

[3] "Ma'am, you cannot say that and expect me just to stand here," Mack whines.

"Then what are you waiting for?" I ask while eyeing his pulsing cock.

I haven't seen two men move so fast in my life. Percy announces they're signing off for the night and thanks the subscribers before shutting the live stream off. Mack's already stalking toward me, pulling his mask off.

"Leave it on," I pretty much beg, hand still on my pussy.

Mack grunts, "No, I have plans for this mouth on that pouty pussy of yours. I'll put it back on later if you want."

---

3. Porn Star - August Alsina

Pulling me up to stand, he grabs the back of my head, immediately smashing his mouth against mine. Our tongues intricately dance together. He doesn't fight for dominance; he is so used to submitting, and that thought alone has me throbbing.

I wrap a fist around his dick, pushing him back toward the couch. I still have my skirt up around my hips, but I've stripped out of everything else. Percy is awkwardly standing beside the front camera. I pull away from Mack. "Are you okay with this, Percy?" I ask, hoping he says yes and joins in.

"More than okay… I want to have some fun too." He's taken his mask off and has his own devilish grin covering his face. "Are you ready for your world to be rocked, Mar?"

With a raised brow, I shoot the question to Mack, "*Papochka's* cocky in the bedroom?"

Mack chuckles. "Of course he is. Look at the monster cock he's carrying around, and let me tell you, he knows how to use it too. But I will say, it's been a while for me since I've been with a woman, so forgive me. I don't know how world-rocking I'm going to be."

Percy comforts him. "We'll talk you through it, Baby Boy. I love you; you know that. And Mar here will let you know what she wants; isn't that right, Mar?"

"Yes, *Luchik*, I'll bring you back to the dark side," I tease, trying to lighten the mood.

Thank fuck Percy knows what he's doing and Mack cares enough to learn and communicate. I'm tired of men not giving a fuck about anyone's pleasure but their own. It's usually me having to rub one out while getting fucked or even after they leave. Let's see how it goes with these two. They're *very* pretty, and the prettier they are, the less they care to learn about pleasing their partners.

You don't see too many pretty men knowing how to fuck.

CHAPTER SIX

@UNTRAINED_GHOSTT

MACK

W e both take Mar by the hand, pulling her toward our bedroom. Percy announces in his deep, seductive voice, "I've wanted you in between us since I laid eyes on you, but laid out on the bed. The couch doesn't have nearly enough room for what I have planned for the three of us."

[1] Percy and I climb up to the center of the bed. Mar is standing at the end, pulling her skirt off slowly. I murmur, "Your body is a sin that I'm willing to drown in, Ma'am."

She has curves that I want to hold onto, and her tits are something I can only thank the Devil herself for creating. Don't get me started on her ass. She's the epitome of a woman. The power she carries and her dominance are the things I'm most envious of, but we find what we need in each other. One thing is for certain—she belongs in control.

She's looking down at us like she's eating this power

---

1. Pretty Little Fears (feat. J. Cole) - 6LACK, J. Cole

dynamic between the three of us right up. "What's the game plan, boys?"

"We figured you knew," I offer up with a shrug. Both of our dicks are still rock-hard, begging to be touched.

Percy was sucking me so good earlier and taking those commands from Mar like a champ. I don't know how I didn't come down his throat while we were live streaming. "Touch each other. I want to watch and see where I fit in," she purrs.

Percy is the first to move; he effortlessly straddles my waist. My hands immediately land on his ass cheeks, spreading him wide open just for Mar. She has a prime view of his tight hole. Crawling up the bed, Mar settles herself behind Percy's back, whispering into his ear, "I'm going to play with that pretty hole of yours, *Papochka*."

His breath hitches, and Percy and I really doubted she would be into the Daddy kink, but she's clearly putting her own spin on it. *Papochka* is "Daddy" in Russian. We figured that out earlier, and he's eating it up. "You love being called *"Papochka,"* don't you?" she's practically growling the question, while reaching around and grabbing his fat cock.

Percy begs, "Yes. Please. More."

"More what, Percy? You're going to have to use better words than that," she urges. He won't get away with his normal bare minimum talking, he gives me.

"You. Mack. I want more of both of you. I can't get enough, and I haven't even had you yet," Percy pants out.

"What? You want a pussy between you two?" she whispers seductively into his ear. She starts nibbling on it while grabbing my cock and jerking both of us together.

I'm not going to last; fuck, this is all way too hot.

"Not just any pussy, yours, only yours," Percy gasps, full-on panting now. This shouldn't make my stomach flip, but it does. I already want her to be ours, but we've made that our line. I'm turning those emotions off… for now.

"Spit on both of your cocks, *Papochka,*" she gives the command effortlessly, and I wince, thinking there is going to be a power battle between these two. But Percy surprises me, doing it immediately. I throw my head back in pleasure as I feel the spit lubricate our cocks. She has both hands around them. I've forgotten how good it can be to add another person to the dynamic. "Mack, grab the lube," she instructs. Reaching over to the bedside table, I grab the black bottle.

She grabs the lube from my hands and uncaps it while I grab the back of Percy's neck and pull him in for a kiss. It heats up quickly, as he bites my bottom lip, I yelp. I hear Mar lubing her fingers up, and the mystery of what she's doing behind Percy makes this even hotter. Light taps on both of my thighs pull me out of my bliss. I follow the unsaid instructions by bending them up as far as I can, which pushes Percy's ass up even further.

"You two ready?" Mar asks, slowly rubbing her hand up my thigh. We both give her quick nods. "Both of you, words, now!" she barks out.

Shit, I forgot. We should know better by this point.

Like we're one person, we both give out a breathy, "Yesss."

"Fuck, I should've brought some toys over. I could be doing all this plus getting myself off," she elaborates like she's just thinking out loud.

Oh, we're getting her off, no questions asked.

She pushes one finger into each of our asses at the same time. I whimper, knowing she loves it so much, and Percy grunts like it took him off guard. "Is this ass sore from getting railed last night, Big Daddy?" It earns her another loud grunt from him. I let out a gasp, feeling her twist her finger around in my ass as she pushes further, making her way to my prostate.

"More, Ma'am, please," I'm really begging now, and I'm absolutely not above it.

"Fuck, beg some more, *Luchik*." She pushes another finger into me and curls them upwards. "You sound like a desperate whore when you're begging me." The moan that escapes me doesn't even sound human. "Is that what you want to be? My dirty little whore?"

Throwing my head back in bliss, but remembering to answer her, I manage, "Mmhmm."

"Grab both of your cocks, Percy." He does, and he spits on them again without Mar even telling him.

"Good boy." I feel him tense for a moment, but he quickly lets go. She's going to have him loving praise in no time.

"I'm a good boy too." I pout, and that earns me another finger. She gives us a couple more slow pumps and then pulls them out.

Now it's Percy's turn to beg, "Mama, please."

"What do you want? To come?" He's bobbing his head up and down.

"Percy, stand up. Mack, I hope to fuck you've eaten pussy before." She already sounds like she has no hope in my skills.

I gasp and grab my chest, faking as if her words have wounded me. "I have, Mar. What do you take me for?" I've fooled around with my fair share of women. It's just been a while.

It's like riding a bike, though, right?

She starts her next command, "Lay horizontal on the bed. I want you to have a view of your boyfriend's cock going down my throat while I suffocate you with this cunt."

She climbs on my face, hovering slightly, and that just

won't do. "Sit the fuck down. Use me. Take what you need," I growl, grabbing her thick thighs and smother myself with her beautiful pussy. "All of it. Smother me, Ma'am, please."

Percy is standing on the bed in front of Mar, and I have the perfect view from down here. She takes his tip into her mouth, pulling back enough to swirl her tongue around the head of his cock. Then she's quick to take all of him, deep into the back of her throat. Looking up, I see him staring down at me, but his eyes bounce between us, not knowing where to look.

"Fuck, Mack, you look so good eating her pussy. How is it?" Percy moans. She's rocking back and forth on my face as she bobs her head up and down Percy's shaft.

She lets out a strangled moan when I shove two fingers into her and I stop sucking her clit to answer, "So, so sweet. I forgot how much I love the taste of pussy. Or maybe it's just yours, Ma'am, and these magnificent tits." I reach up with my free hand and grab a handful, pinching and twisting her nipple.

Percy grunts out, "I'm fucking these beautiful tits eventually, Mama."

It feels so good to have her between us like this, like it's where she's meant to be—but that's delusional, right? I just met Mar, but our fantasies are coming alive, and we have so many more already planned. Mar and I are bringing Percy's to life tonight if everything works out. And I have a feeling it will tie us together, whether we like it or not.

She's close. I can feel her pussy squeezing my fingers. She starts grinding faster on my face, using me just like I told her to. I curl my fingers and give one hard suck to her clit, and she's pushed right off the edge, letting out a scream as she stops sucking Percy's cock. She's looking down at me in awe, so I ask her, "How'd I do?"

[2] "So, so good, *Luchik*. Such a good boy." She leans down, giving me a soft kiss. As we get lost in the kiss for a minute, I feel Percy set himself behind Mar. She moves to get on her hands and knees. "I want someone in my pussy and someone fucking my mouth. I don't care who's where, but I'm getting spit-roasted."

I scoot up the bed, getting to my knees, positioning myself in front of her mouth. Percy firmly places his hands on her luscious hips and pulls her ass cheeks apart. She looks back at him; he's biting his lip as he breathes in a lungful of air. "You like what you see, Big Daddy?" She taunts Percy with a shake of her ass which earns her a slap that has her groaning.

"That's a pretty pussy, ain't it, Percy?" I ask, knowing exactly how pretty that cunt is.

"Are you going to just stare at it? C'mon, it won't bite," Mar barks out, shaking her ass one more time. Unexpectedly, she takes me deep to the back of her throat. Hissing out, I grab the sides of her head—I'm so sensitive, but that's not going to stop me. I shove into her deeper. She tries to smile with a mouth full of my dick, and I smirk back at her, as the tears start to gather in her eyes.

I hear Percy spit. "You ready, Mar?" Percy asks.

"Yes. Fuck me. Now," she commands.

He wastes no time, inserting his bare head up against her waiting pussy and shoving his way in. I have the ideal view of Percy entering her. He throws his head back in bliss. She gasps, clawing at my thighs, but still sucking me.

He pauses once he's balls deep. "Fuucckkk," Percy growls. He pulls back and slams back into her even harder. His big balls are making a hard slapping noise against her,

---

2. OHMAMI - With Maggie Lindeman - Chase Atlantic, Maggie Lindeman

and it's music to my ears. Mar tries to reach down to rub her clit, but Percy smacks her hand away before she gets to it.

He reaches down and slowly starts to rub her clit in heavy-pressured circles while fucking her like a menace. I hear Percy spit again, drawing my attention, and this time he's looking right at me.

Knowing exactly what he's thinking, I instruct him, "Let's fill that last hole, Daddy." Mar reaches up, cups my balls, and starts tugging on them. Percy's thumb breaches her back hole. "You look like a menace right now, Percy. God, you really know how to fuck." I yell—fuck, what the hell? That hurt! I pull Mar off my cock and look down at her. "What the hell was that for?" She just pulled on my balls so hard.

She tilts her head, questioning me, "God's not with us. Who is?"

"The damn Devil and she just yanked on my fucking balls." I give her a hateful look, but it only lasts until she gets my cock back in her mouth.

"We're taking you at the same time—eventually. Not tonight, but it will happen, Mar. Right now, we're going to work these tight little holes up to it," Percy grits out while hammering into her, announcing every word with each thrust.

"You going to come for us, Sovereign?" I hiss as I rock into her throat. She's an incoherent, slobbering mess, but taking exactly what she wants. "Keep throwing that luscious ass back on my boyfriend's cock. Yessss, just like that." I'm full-on face-fucking her now. "Mmm. I don't know where to look. Should I look at your face getting stuffed with my cock or at Daddy filling you up so perfect-ly?" That immediately sets her off; she pulls off my cock, and she comes with a scream. Wait, she's not just coming... she's squirting all over Percy.

She quickly gets up and scoots away from us. I imagine it's because she's so sensitive now, but now I can lick her cum off of Percy. She's on a different planet and murmurs, "I just squirted..." She looks genuinely confused and adds, "I have tried everything, and I've never been able to make it happen."

"Goddamn, that was hot as fuck," Percy hums, still looking shocked that he could pull that out of her.

She's sprawled out with her stomach facing down on the bed.

We still haven't been able to come, and I hope she doesn't edge us for the rest of the night. She cuts me off from my thoughts and casually throws out, "Sixty-nine and come down each other's throats." We lay ourselves sideways beside her and start mindlessly sucking each other off. "Mmm, I love watching my two little sluts please one another."

"You taste so good, Ma'am," I call out, licking up and down Percy's cock. A couple of grunts and moans later, and we're both shooting down each other's throats. I swallow Percy greedily. Then, panting out, "That is the most edging I've had happen in a while."

She gives Percy one last command, "Hold it, Percy. Don't swallow. I want his cum after all."

She lays down beside him, and he opens his mouth, letting my cum slowly drip into her mouth. It takes everything in me not to groan at the sight.

"Mmm, you taste like sin, *Luchik*." She reaches up and pulls Percy in for a heated kiss. "My good boys."

"Fuck, please stop. I can't get hard again," I whine.

"We're going out tonight and coming back to partake in more of that," she says as she shoots me a wink. I already know what she's thinking, and we have a very special treat up our sleeves for Percy.

"Oh, I know there will be plenty more of what just happened. You're not getting rid of us after that performance," Percy promises.

She shrugs. "Another fantasy checked off for me. Actually two. Squirting and being spit-roasted."

* * *

We pile into the back of the ride-share and head to the strip. Mar and I decided to head to Club Onyx. It's brand new and looks like a complete vibe from what I've seen on social media. It has the perfect spots for pictures, and the inside is covered in seductive red lighting. We didn't tell Percy where we were going, trying to keep everything a surprise.

I had a dress, heels, basic makeup items, and jewelry delivered to the house earlier. I called the girl who does my hair, Blair, to get recommendations on makeup. She sent me a huge cart from one of the makeup stores to order and pick up.

I told Mar she was beautiful without it, but I wanted her to have some handy because, according to her social media, it looked like she dabbled with it. I picked out a little black velvet-type dress with off-the-shoulder sleeves that make her chest look marvelous. It's ruched on the ass, which accentuates it perfectly. I guessed her size, and by the looks of it, it fits her body like a glove. The heels have black straps around the ankles and a single strap over the toes. The jewelry I bought puts the finishing touches on her aesthetic with some gold hoop earrings and a dainty necklace.

We walk through the doors, past the bouncers outside.

The hallway is lined with these gold oval-looking plates from floor to ceiling, and the red lighting is doing something to me. At the end of the hall, there is a red neon sign that says "SINNER." The eclectic vibe in here reminds me of my shop and the house.

"Picture time!" Mar sing songs to both of us.

"We don't have our masks on." Percy sounds the least bit excited.

"I'll make it work. Come on, old man." She grabs both of us by the hands and drags us to the end of the hall. She asks a girl standing close to the sign if she minds taking a picture for us. She still has her glowing red horns on; they're a part of her at this point.

She stands facing the camera. We come up to stand by her sides, and she tells us to turn toward the sign so you can only see the sides of our faces illuminated by the red lights. She wraps her arms around each of our waists. "Now turn and face the camera. I want one of all of us, just for me," she remarks.

"I think that's the nicest thing you've said all day, Mar," Percy states dryly, being the smartass he is.

"What, you didn't think my praise while I was squirting all over you earlier was nice?" she says, and I swear he chokes on his tongue.

That's what his smartass gets.

The poor girl taking the pictures is blushing so deeply. "Yeah, to you. She's been nice to me all day—besides the hand stomping. Which was hot as fuck, if you ask me." The girl behind the camera is going to burst into flames.

Looking at the pictures, we're smiling down at Mar, like two lost fools, ready to take any command she'll give us.

CHAPTER
SEVEN

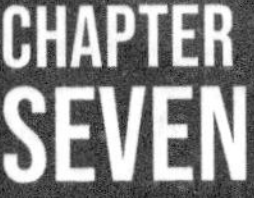

@KÖNIGOFTHEUNDERWORLD
PERCY

Stepping foot into the club, I see how breathtaking it is in here. Club Onyx has been open for about two months now. I haven't been in here since it opened to the public. I do the marketing for the owner, Marcello Barone, who is the head of the Italian Mafia. Anyone who lives in Vegas is aware of Mr. Barone and his family business.

Why does the Don need marketing?

Well, he runs a shit ton of businesses and likes for them to do well, so he outsourced to the company I work for. He'll only work with me, though. No one else at the firm wants anything to do with his "dirty money." As for me, money's money. The marketing for all of his legal busi-nesses is easy, so I don't mind. He offers me a scary amount of money to leave my current firm and work for him at least once a month, but I haven't made the jump yet.

He scares the shit out of me if I'm being completely honest.

Contrary to what you would think, Marcello has been nothing but nice to me, and I'm excited to introduce him to Mack and Mar. He was very specific about this project, almost like he really didn't need me to work on it as much. He didn't seem to care how well the club does.

My attention floats back to Mar. She already fits so well into our partnership, and we've known her for less than twenty-four hours. That should worry me, but in all honesty, it doesn't. I have some sort of pull toward her. It was nice earlier to let go of the power and submit to her, taking all her commands. Submission comes easily to Mack, but I've always held back and fought when submitting to him… but not with Mar. She leaves no questions about who's in charge.

They're in front of me, heading up to the bar. Mack's arm is slung over her shoulder, and hers over his hip. I can't help but appreciate the differences in their bodies. Her hips are swaying in that tight velvet dress, and Mack's back in that white button-down has blood rushing straight to my cock.

She's soft and curvy.

He's pure muscle.

I really do have the best of both worlds with these two.

At the bar, I step up behind them, wrapping my hands possessively around their waists, not caring about what people think. Mar orders all our drinks, and I think it's something with tequila.

I should've seen her as a tequila girl.

The bartender comes back, setting all our cups on the bar, but I'm distracted by Mack's hand running down my stomach toward my dick. He steps in front of me, laying kisses all over my neck, nibbling and throwing in a little suck here and there. As Mack gives me all his attention, I feel Mar shove a drink into my hands.

Our hips begin to sway to the music. If we run into him tonight, I'll have to compliment Marcello on his DJ.

Speaking of the Devil, and I don't mean the one in

front of me either. Marcello walks up beside me, and I open my mouth to introduce Mack and Mar, but before I can, he barks out, "Marfa. What the hell are you doing in my fucking club?" His hand goes to the Glock in his waistband. She snaps her head around, and when her eyes land on Marcello, she's immediately pissed off.

How the fuck does he know her? My protective guard goes up immediately, and I step in front of her slightly.

"Marcello, hello. How are you tonight?" Reaching out a hand for him to shake. He glances at my hand, his eyes finding Mar's again—the look of pure hatred in his eyes.

"You know any Russian under your father's thumb cannot be in any business of mine," he spits. Mack is completely lost right now. I'm honestly right there with him. "Let alone his flesh and blood," he sneers in disgust.

So, Mar's dad and Marcello don't get along… but why does that involve Mar?

"Someone, please fill me in," Mack pleads. He leans in loud enough for all of us to hear but whispers, "Mar, he looks scary as fuck." She puts up her hand to silence him.

"You know I'm not an Abdulov anymore. Why'd you get your guard dog to fire me, Barone? He owns the place. I didn't know he took orders like a whipped bitch. Were you too afraid to confront me yourself?" How the fuck is she not shitting herself talking to him like this? Marcello is a scary fucking man. He always looks one minor inconvenience away from taking his Glock out of his waistband, and would find joy blowing your brains out. I don't want to be on the receiving end of that.

Ever.

"Because you should never have been working at Sins." Marcello doesn't own Sins, but he has all the power over this city and well beyond. I don't know who they're referring to. I remember the owner chatting with me once about maybe taking over his marketing for Sins, but nothing ever came of it.

It would be cool as fuck to have a sex club in my marketing portfolio, but I need to figure out why he let Mar go. I could tell it hurt her to lose that job when she was telling us about it earlier today.

"I got the job there, fair and square. I didn't know Vincent was your paid psycho killer," she spits in disgust.

Vincent.

I remember shaking his hand in a couple of meetings with Marcello, but I'm clearly not immersed in the mafia side of his business. Vincent was always standing in the background, begging someone to do something stupid.

"We've had some big issues with your piece-of-shit father. I'm not going to risk Vincent employing you and having insider information. Anything or anyone that threatens someone I care about, you're immediately out, if not dead." I don't miss that threat.

"You know I hate my dad. I would never side with that man." She almost sounds hurt that he would think that.

"That's your blood. I don't care how much you say you hate him. He could hold something over your head. You know he would do that. He's slimy. You're not going to have access to anything Italian-owned. End of discussion."

I'm turning my head back and forth, waiting for the next thing to be said.

"So, your dad is the head of the Russian mafia?" Mack asks, still not understanding that this is not the time or place to be asking these kinds of questions—especially in front of Marcello. I do not want to be on that man's kill list; no, thank you. I hit Mack in the stomach and look at him with the most "please shut the fuck up" eyes I can muster.

Marcello finally looks over at me. "Percy, nice to see you here."

"I would say the same, but you're treating Mar like she's a piece of trash." Fuck, I can't believe I just said that to him.

"You'll watch your mouth," Marcello grits out.

"No, he won't," Mar grits out in return.

Ensuring her it's ok, I say, "Mar, it's fine."

"No, it's not. He's going to learn that not everyone bows down to him." Fuck she's so hot like this.

"They do, though… at least I do," I say back to her. I'm really not trying to start shit. "He's a client of mine. We've known each other for a couple of years."

"Okay, even more reason for him not to be all high and mighty with you. It's distasteful, Marcello. Now apologize." He's squeezing his fist so hard his knuckles are turning white.

I don't think he's going to, but to my surprise, he barely manages to say, "I'm sorry, Percy." With that, I throw my whole drink back. I'm over this wild shit.

"You've all got about three songs, and I don't want to see you in my club anymore," he exclaims while looking right at Mar.

[1] Not wasting any more time, we head out to the dance floor. We have Mar between us, and her hands are roaming all over Mack while she's grinding and rubbing her ass all over my cock. This is what these two wanted to do tonight —shake their asses. Well, I hope they're having a good time.

That's the last thought I have before everything goes black.

____

1. Buy U a Drank (Shawty Snappin') (feat. Yung Joc) - T-Pain, Yung Joc

I grunt, picking up Percy, then throw him over my shoulder. He was just about to be laid out on the dance floor, but I caught him right as I saw his eyes rolling back into his head. "You better be glad I hit the gym every day," I say, smirking at Mar. I can't believe we're doing this right now. Mar would have croaked if she had seen me googling the risks and things to look out for when giving someone Rohypnol. We literally just roofied my boyfriend.

What the actual fuck is wrong with us?

I mean, he wanted this, but it still feels so wrong…

I should probably be worried that she knew exactly where to get the drug to do this, but Percy's getting to live out his fantasy, so I shut those thoughts down. Who am I to ask questions? I didn't think she was still going to go through with it after the run-in with the scary mafia man, but it was too late once she gave Percy his drink.

Setting him down in the back of a ride share, I assure the concerned looking driver, "He had a little too much fun tonight." It would be a different story if it were Mar who was passed the fuck out, but she's bright-eyed and ready to go.

Getting Percy into the house is a task. I put him on the couch and slip his shirt off while he's sitting up. Then, I slowly lay him down and turn around to get the cameras set up. We're just filming this one, not live-streaming it. It would be reported, especially with him not being coherent. We'll probably have to put a clip at the beginning of the video of Percy giving his consent, along with copious trigger warnings.

Percy had mentioned earlier that this fantasy was the ultimate version of him giving up his control, which makes total sense now. I catch myself checking on him every couple of seconds to make sure he's still breathing. He's totally fine; dare I say, he even looks peaceful. I have no clue how we're going to do this. Now I'm wondering if Percy is even going to be able to get his cock hard while being knocked the fuck out.

Guess we'll see.

[1] Mar walks in, looking more devilish than ever. I let out a whistle and shoot her a wink as we lock eyes. Fuck, I haven't felt like this over a woman in a minute. She makes my stomach flip in the best way possible.

"Is everything ready? I wouldn't even know where to start with setting all this shit up. Your entire setup is way more intricate than mine is," she says. This has me wondering what hers is like and if she has everything she needs. I want to take care of her. I want to keep her, but Percy specifically told me that we couldn't get attached to her, and I know he meant that just for me. But I haven't missed the way he's been looking at her either.

It might be too late for that, especially after tonight.

---

1. STRANGER THINGS - Chase Atlantic

"Yes, everything is ready to go. I just have to get my mask on." She walks up to me, reaches out, wraps a hand around my throat, and pulls me down to her lips. I'm grinning so hard. I love being choked, but she's not applying a ton of pressure; she's just holding me where she wants me.

She teases me as she hovers over my lips, brushing hers along mine, whispering, "Do you like being choked, *Luchik*?"

My cock jumps in my pants. I'm smiling and bobbing my head up and down.

"I'll keep that in mind, but only if you're a good boy tonight." I love her dirty talk so much. I know Percy does, too. "Put his mask on, too, while you're at it. I wonder if they're going to know he's out of it in the beginning," Mar states while her eyes roam over his naked stomach and chest. He looks edible. I didn't think I had a somnophilia kink, but here I am with my cock straining against my zipper. I don't really know if it's Mar's hand around my throat or if seeing Percy like this is doing it to me.

I say, thinking out loud, "I'm sure they'll figure it out pretty quick. It feels weird not doing this one live."

Leaning down and picking up the back of Percy's head, I slide his mask on. I whisper into Percy's ear, "You're getting exactly what you want, aren't you, Daddy?"

I swear, I see his cock jump in his slacks as I'm pulling my mask in place.

"So, I researched this. It pretty much says he can stay hard as long as he's dreaming or remembering previous sexual experiences," Mar says with the straightest face, like this is a casual conversation.

"Okay, so what do we have to do?" This is the craziest thing I've ever done.

"Pretty much the more dirty talk, the better. It's going to put him in that headspace of having sexual things happening to him. We need to get that fat cock of his rock hard and up, then keep it that way."

We both look down at the same time. His cock's straining against his pants already.

I chuckle. "Well, that was easier than I thought it would be."

"You two don't have any weed lying around, do you? I like to smoke a little before; it makes the orgasms even better, and the creativity to fuck with you all flows even more than it already is," She asks.

"Of course we do. What do you take us for, prudes?" I run and grab a blunt out of my side drawer inside my nightstand. Pulling my mask up where it's just sitting on top of my head, I light it and inhale while walking back into the living room. I hand it over to Mar with a smirk. "Why didn't you tell us before that you liked to smoke?"

"I don't like getting judged about it, so I usually keep it to myself until I know I can trust the person." Her trusting us shouldn't make my stomach flip out of excitement, but it does.

She trusts us.

I'm smiling like a fool, and she's looking at me like I am one. She inhales and holds it for a couple of seconds. She then blows it out into my face, and I can't wait to see how good this is about to be.

I turn the speaker on at a low volume and press play on our streaming playlist. [1] I want the subscribers to be able to hear all the nasty shit we're about to feed Percy's psyche. I'm sliding my mask back on my face and walking to the first camera. I hit record before doing the same with the second.

I hate the process of filming, editing, and doing all the extra shit that comes along with recording. With live streaming, you don't have to worry about all the extras. It'll be worth it, since Percy's darkest fantasy is coming to life.

Finally done with all the setup, I turn to Mar and seductively ask, "Where do you want me, Mommy?"

"Don't make me like the Mommy shit, please; I don't need any more kinks," she says with a laugh, masking her breathing that's picking up slightly.

Hmm, she likes that… I'll keep that in mind for next time.

We're still dressed in our clothes from the club. As she bends over at the hip to take her shoes off, I can't stop the

---

1. Unholy (feat. Kim Petras) - Sam Smith, Kim Petras

groan that leaves me, causing her to look back at me. "Sovereign, that ass is going to kill me… At least I'll go to hell a happy man." Kneeling down, I grab the strap to the heel she's working on undoing. Slowly, I pull it off, then offer to help with the other. "Here, let me."

"Ghost, you know I love you on your knees," she purrs, looking down at me. Her red, glowing horns are still seated on her head. She really never takes those things off.

"Get that pretty pussy out for me, then." I help her step out of her shoes as she pulls her dress up. Of course, this woman doesn't have any underwear on. "Where's the underwear that I bought you, Sovereign?"

"I don't know, *Luchik;* you tell me." She smirks down at me while reaching out and grabbing the top of my head by my hair and the spandex material that covers it. Groaning, I let her pull me to where I've wanted to be all night.

"König, or should I say, *Papochka?* I've got your sweet little boyfriend's tongue in my pussy."

I lap at her clit, nice and slow, only to pull away and say, "Please, get those big tits out for me, Ma'am. I'll have the view of a lifetime from down here on my knees for you."

"It's a shame… If your boyfriend was awake, he would be down there with you." I reach over and run my hand down Percy's tight stomach, trailing down to his V-line, and palm his cock through his pants. With my other hand, I push two fingers into Mar's pussy. Wanting this orgasm to hit her fast and hard, I relentlessly suck her clit into my mouth and move my fingers back and forth. She's still standing, looking down at me. "Fuck, Ghost, yesss, harrrdderrr."

That's all I need to keep going. She's grinding her lush hips back and forth on my face while squeezing my fingers deep inside her, trying to rub that spot that I know will send her over the edge.

"You're almost there, aren't you? Drown me, Sovereign." I pick up my speed with my hand, back and forth, back and forth, practically shaking her whole body. Then bite down on her throbbing clit.

As her orgasm hits her, she squirts all over my face and down my chest. "Fuucckkk! I'm coming, Ghost! Fuck, fuck, fuck!"

As she's coming down from the high, I start unbuttoning Percy's pants. She's quick to join me, and pulls his pants down his ass and legs while I shift his weight around. Mar climbs onto the couch and sits between his open legs, facing me, while I'm on my knees. She spreads her legs and motions for me to come to where she is with her fingers.

"Look at him. Rock hard and knocked out. Worthless and helpless. How about you suck his cock? Get it nice and wet for me. I'm going to ride that defenseless dick." His cock is jumping at Mar's words, leaking and so swollen. I know it's painful, but he's about to have the ride of his life.

With one hand she's rubbing her clit. Then she's using her other hand to lift my mask just enough so my mouth is visible, and I suck two of her fingers into my mouth to wet them. She pulls them out of my mouth, immediately lowering them into her pussy while simultaneously rubbing her clit. With both hands on her plump pussy, it's pushing her gorgeous tits up on display.

"Ma'am, you look so good fucking that dripping cunt with your fingers." I take the head of Percy's dick into my mouth, paying special attention to the slit. Lapping up any pre-cum that has seeped out, I moan, "He tastes so good."

"What's he taste like, Ghost?" she questions me, and I don't know which name I like better. Ghost, or whatever the hell she calls me in Russian.

I moan, "He tastes like sin… And I *don't* wanna to be a saint."

Taking him into the back of my throat, I give him a couple of deep bobs of my head and twist of my hand over his shaft. He lets out the sexiest whimper that I've ever heard come from him.

"Did you hear that? He loves his helpless cock being sucked. I'm about to use it like my favorite fucktoy," Mar says while she watches me take Percy into the back of my throat, all while she's still rubbing and fucking that perfect pussy of hers.

She gets to her knees, and I release his cock to run my hand over Mar's clit. It's right there—swollen and begging me to pay it some more attention. She straddles Percy, and I line his cock up with her tight cunt as she takes a seat. "Mmm, you feel that, *Papochka*. This cunt wrapping around you. Even while you're drugged up and living out your fantasy."

I stand up and lean over, making my way to Percy's mouth. I pull up his mask so I have access to the bottom half of his face. I don't know if this is going to work, but we're going to test it out. I turn his head to the side and open his mouth for him. Lowly, I whisper to Percy, "You're going to suck your boyfriend's cock, König.

Mar reaches down, rubbing her clit back and forth as she grinds on Percy, taking exactly what she needs from him. I encourage her, "Look at you, greedy with your orgasms. Are you going to come on his worthless dick?" I'm not much of a degrader, but sometimes, it comes out of me by surprise.

Switch energy and all that.

"Fuck, he feels so good. I shouldn't be enjoying this," I say as I push my cock into his mouth little by little. It's almost like he is sucking subconsciously.

"You think he's going to be able to come?" Mar questions.

"I would think so. He's rock-hard. Then again, I've never drugged and fucked someone before."

With a wicked laugh, Mar states, "Neither have I."

"You haven't fucked me yet, Ghost. König, you want to be able to re-watch your boyfriend fuck me for the first time whenever you want?" She pauses for dramatic effect. "Oh, that was a yes, okay, perfect," she answers for Percy, which has me chuckling.

"How about you fuck me from the back, and I can suck König's dick?" I move over behind her once she's off the couch. She has her knees on the floor, her arms hanging over Percy's waist, swirling her tongue around his cock. My dick's pulsating just from the sight of her being on her knees, licking her own juices off of him.

"This fucking ass," I groan, grabbing it up in my hands. "Daddy, I bet you wish you were awake to see this. Good thing it's getting filmed. You get to see your darkest desires come to life." She pushes back on my hand. "Are you ready, Ma'am? Or should I say, Mommyyy?" A moan slips out when I say, "Mommy," and she whimpers.

I'd say that's a yes.

Fuck, I could get used to hearing that.

"Just fuck me, Ghost," Mar spits. Percy's cock starts to twitch, and I know for a fact he can hear what's going on. I really hope he's enjoying this and not having some nightmare or bad trip.

I line my cock up to her pussy and sink right in with no warning. I start to fuck her hard and fast it's causing her to push down further and further, making her gag on Percy's cock.

I run my hand up and down her back before circling

my arm around her to find her clit. "I want you coming on my cock at least once, Ma'am."

[2]"Harder, Ghost, fuck my pussy like it's the last one you'll ever have."

It is the last one I'll ever have.

Goddamnit, I can't be doing this right now. We've known she's existed for almost twenty-four hours. I. Can. Not. Get. Attached. She doesn't want that.

In between thrusts, I pant out, "König, I wish you could see this Devil choking on your fat cock. Do you feel that, Daddy? Her drool's running down onto those balls. Fuck, Mar, get his ass ready. I have to have it tonight." She slows, releasing Percy, and grabs the lube to soak her fingers. She starts with one finger and then is quick to work another in.

"Damn, I wish I had my toys here. We would have so many more options," she exclaims.

Before I can stop myself, I blurt out, "Can you bring them over next time?"

You dumbass, there could be no next time.

This pay-per-view is probably going to blow up, and I'm sure she'll get what she needs and go on her merry way.

But I don't want her to go.

"Do you want me to peg you, *Luchik*?" An involuntary whimper crawls out of me, but I still get out a "yes."

Still pounding into her from the back, I start to speed up and add more pressure to that swollen little clit. "Come on my cock, Sovereign. I want your cum slicking my dick up to fuck König's ass." That takes her right over the edge. Grinding my teeth, pulling out of her, and grabbing my cock at the base, I somehow hold back my orgasm.

---

2. Swervin (feat. 6ix9ine) - A Boogie Wit da Hoodie, 6ix9ine

Mar slowly comes down from her orgasm, and I move up to the couch to get Percy situated for the next thing I have in mind. "I've only ever seen this done in porn, but I think it's going to work. "I'm going to pull his legs up to his chest, but you'll keep them wide, almost to his sides. His dick's going to have to be pulled down between his legs toward both of us. I need full access to his ass, so a pillow is going under. It's going to be a tight fit... but hot as fuck."

"I already know this is going to be the best thing I've ever seen. Thank fuck, we're recording this. Permanent spank bank material." I chuckle at her, truly never knowing what she's going to say.

We begin to move into position, but I pick Mar up and put her right over Percy's lap. She has Percy's legs up by his chest, causing him to look like a dead bug.

Mar holds onto his ankles, facing away from me, as I get myself situated. She leans back as I line up his cock to her entrance, and she sits down, taking him all the way to the hilt. She lets out a soft sigh like she's missed him being inside of her.

I know that feeling.

"König, how's that pussy feeling? It's been a while since you've been in one. Well, on camera, that is." I shoot a wink at the camera because he was balls-deep in Mar earlier.

Gripping both of her ass cheeks in appreciation, I growl, "Fuck, I love these curves."

I use my lubed fingers to stretch Percy's hole out. Even though he's passed out, I don't want to risk hurting him by going in with no prep, and Mar's fingers have been out of him too long. "Daddy, you're so relaxed for me. Sovereign has your cock in her cunt, so deep, and I have two of my fingers in this snug ass of yours. Getting it nice and ready for me." I take a deep breath, trying to ready myself to be inside of him, then keep depicting, "His ass is squeezing my fingers so tight; I think he's ready for me now."

I lube up my cock, being extra careful and making sure I don't hurt him. I grab him under his ass and pull him up even more. "Ma'am, hold still while I ease into him. There's no way he's going to last long with how good we're about to make him feel. Using him like the little fuckdoll he is." I line myself up and push my tip in, popping past his tight ring of muscle. He lets out the quietest of noises in appreciation.

"He whimpers so pretty," Mar groans.

She starts to bounce on Percy's dick. I have the perfect view of her plump ass is moving up and down. Each time she meets his thighs, it ripples. "I usually can't see how perfectly his cock fills my holes. Now I get to watch him fuck your holes… I think this might be my new favorite thing."

"I want your cum deep in me, *Papochka*," she pants out while enunciating her next words breathlessly.

"Every." Riding up and slamming back down.

"Last." She moves her hand to her clit.

"Drop." I reach around her to pinch both of her nipples between my fingers.

Moaning, I say, "König, your ass is squeezing me so hard. You're drugged and helpless. Getting used like the fucktoy you always wished to be." I'm hammering into him so hard, and Mar is riding at the same speed. Fuck, maybe he won't be able to come.

"Too bad we had to drug your ass to get you to give up full control." Mar starts grinding back and forth. "Fuck, *Luchik, Papochka*. I'm coming," she yelps before she comes on a scream.

Percy's ass is suffocating me, pulsating, and taking me over the edge, right behind her. Pulling Mar against my chest, I groan into her neck as I come, "Sovereign, Daddy."

Mar looks over her shoulder at me with a smug grin. "We got him to come." She lifts herself from Percy's dick, and his cum is dripping out of her right back onto his cock. As she climbs off, I pull out of him gently.

Pulling my mask up just enough to free my mouth, I lean down and take his cock into my mouth. "Mmm, can't miss out on my boyfriend's cum." She grabs me again by my throat, pulling me to her.

She leans in and licks both my lips. "We do taste good together, Ghost." I'm speechless, staring into her eyes.

I snap out of it, and I am up, stopping the recordings on both cameras. I cannot wait to re-watch this. Hopefully, Percy wants to tomorrow, and I'm praying to the Devil beside me that he doesn't regret wanting us to do this to him.

I hear the water running in our bathroom attached to the master bedroom. Mar must be getting it ready. I shouldn't be giddy about that, but here I am picking up my big-ass boyfriend, carrying him into the tub that she's already sitting in to give Percy the aftercare he's going to need. With the biggest smile on my face, I sit us on the opposite side of the oversized tub. She scoots over to our side so we're all back-to-chest in silence until the water gets cold. We wash Percy, then ourselves, before we dry him off together and get him into bed.

Mar and I are drifting off to sleep as our heads hit the pillows. Percy lies in the middle, cherished and cared for—like I've always wished he'd let me do for him when it was just the two of us.

@KÖNIGOFTHEUNDERWORLD
PERCY

I wake up with the worst headache I've had since my college days. Fuck, my mouth is dry, and I may have been ran over by an eighteen-wheeler with the way my body is feeling. Trying to get my wits about me, as I'm peeling my eyes open.

What the fuck happened last night?

I'm in our bed, and when I roll over to my other side, I'm met with a body, but it's not Mack… there are no tattoos. My eyes land on the hair, and that gives her away. It's Mar, sleeping soundly.

What the hell is going on? I didn't see her as the staying-over type, so we must've gotten plastered last night. The last thing I remember is talking with a pissed-off Marcello, and it's all black after that. I can't even tell you how I got home.

Looking over Mar, I see that Mack's not in here. I start to panic a little. Did he make it home? What if we left him at the club? Did Marcello's crazy ass do something to him? What the fuck is happening?

I sit up and swing my legs over the side of the bed, but

I am immediately hit with a wave of nausea. Running to the bathroom that's attached to our room, I dry-heave until my stomach is cramping.

I need to find Mack. With all the strength left in me, I get up a lot slower this time, trying to keep the sickness at bay. Walking into the kitchen, turning the corner, I see Mack standing there looking chipper as ever. He is shaking his ass to the music playing, as he's cooking a massive breakfast spread.

[1] Letting out a breath I didn't know I was holding, I sigh, "Thank fuck, you're okay. I thought Marcello had done something bad to you." Wrapping my hands around his waist, I plaster my chest to his back. At this moment, I realize I couldn't, and never want to, live without him. He really is my soul mate.

"Percy, nothing happened to me. It was you that we drugged and took advantage of." He shoots me a wink, and my breath hitches. Did he just say what I think he did? There's no way in hell those two pulled that off on their own.

It is Mar and Mack, though…

I think we were on the dance floor… the only thing bouncing around in my head is Marcello being pissed at Mar for being in his club. "Did we figure out why Marcello was so mad? I've never seen him like that. Quite frankly, I never want to see him like that ever again."

"Something about Mar's dad being the head of the Russian Bravata, and I guess he's Italian… Mafia? I'm not really sure. I was trying not to piss myself… Marcello's scary." I chuckle at that. He's not lying; Marcello is scary as fuck, but I think he would've done something last night if he really wanted to. Nothing happened, and if I remember

---

1. in these walls (my house) (feat. PVRIS) - Machine Gun Kelly, PVRIS

correctly, he even let us get a couple of songs in on the dance floor.

I fill Mack in, "He's one of my major clients. The biggest one, actually. I've never seen that side of him. We need to ask Mar more about it."

Mar comes around the corner into the kitchen. "Ask me more about what?" She's breathtaking, even right out of bed. She has one of Mack's T-shirts on, which swallows her whole, reaching halfway down her thighs. I'm secretly hoping she doesn't have anything under there.

Not the time to get hard, Percy.

"Marcello," Mack answers. "But really, we're not skimming over the fact that we made your darkest fantasy come to life last night. We have the footage of it all, too. Come on, I know you want to see it." He nudges me on the shoulder while flipping the bacon in the pan. How he cooks bacon with no shirt on, I'll never know.

[2] "How do you feel?" Mar asks, looking right into my eyes. I try not to look away, but I do. Embarrassment floods me; I shouldn't have wanted this. My fantasy was too dark and out of hand already, but then I wanted it filmed so I could relive it whenever I want. Plus, wanting to profit off of it…

God, I'm fucked up.

"Hey, look at me." She moves in front of me, her chest hitting my stomach, and her hands come to my face. She has such a dominant personality that I truly forget how little her frame is. "I don't want to see that ashamed look again. I see it written all over your face. We all have our fantasies, Percy. Yours is just a little darker than most, but it was beyond hot. I can't wait for us to put it on the TV and

---

2. Going Bad (feat. Drake) - Meek Mill, Drake

watch it with you." My cock's already straining in my gray sweatpants, and my ass is deliciously sore.

I spin on my heel, and question, "Mack, did you fuck me last night?"

"I don't know, Daddy. You'll have to watch and see." With a smirk on his face, he finishes cooking everything, plates it all, and brings it to us on the couch. We dive in, groaning at how good it all tastes.

Mar moans, shoving food into her mouth like she hasn't eaten in days. "Mack, how can you be that hot and know how to cook?" Now that I'm thinking of it… when was the last time we ate? I think it was the takeout last night.

He just shrugs. "Are you both ready to watch this? If it gets to be too much, Percy, tell us, and we'll turn it off." I nod, and the screen fills with Mack on his knees, taking Mar's heels off from last night. There I am, passed out cold, mask on, lying on the couch behind them.

You probably wouldn't know just by glancing at the video that I was out cold, but then I hear Mar's voice coming through the speakers, *"Look at him. Rock hard and knocked the fuck out. Worthless and helpless. How about you suck his cock? Get it nice and wet for me. I'm going to ride that defenseless dick."*

There's no way in hell I'm going to watch this without having my cock in my hand. Mar's dirty talk is top-tier. I look over at both of them beside me; they're looking back at me, waiting for my reaction. "I'm hard as a rock right now. I'm fine with this—more than fine, actually. I don't know how much longer I can go without having my dick in my hand." I practically moan, as the nausea I felt earlier goes right out the window.

Mar gets down on her knees in front of the couch and crawls over to me. Hands running up my thighs, she palms my cock in my sweats. She drags her hands up toward the waistband of my pants, freeing my cock. It points straight at her, begging to be in her mouth. I really want to watch her, but I can't take my eyes off the TV, with the need to know exactly what they did to me last night and hear every single filthy word that came out of their mouths.

"Watch and let us take care of you, *Papochka*. We can make you feel good… just like we did last night. I don't want you coming until Mack allows you to, okay?" she instructs while taking my cock to the back of her throat. No teasing or lead-up. Mack grabs the side of my face and pulls me into a searing kiss. I melt into the kiss momentarily, and then my attention is pulled back to the TV.

"Do you want me to peg you, Luchik?"

I look at Mack and whine, "Did she peg you last night, and I missed it?"

"No, she didn't have her toys with her, but she's bringing them next time," he responds with the utmost enthusiasm.

Mar's looking up at me with my cock still in her mouth, shooting me a wink. Goddamn, she's still so powerful even with my cock stretching that hot, wet mouth of hers. I see Mack moving out of the corner of my eye. He runs his hands down Mar's back and slides himself behind her. He flips her T-shirt up and exposes her bare ass. I let out an unashamed groan. "Fuck, Mar, your ass is to die for… honestly your whole body is perfect," I say, running my hand over her face. She takes me all the way to the back of her throat once again, gagging with spit running down her chin and onto my balls.

Pulling my attention away from how she's working me, I look back up at the screen. Now it's Mack's voice in the video. *"König, I wish you could see this Devil choking on your fat cock. Do you feel that, Daddy? Her drool's running down onto those balls. Fuck, Mar, get his ass ready. I have to have it tonight."* That was hot, and the fact that I'm watching it and it's being done to me is almost too much. They have this rushed sense in the video, I can feel their need through the screen.

The subscribers are going to eat this shit up.

I confide, "It's even better right now, Mack. She's doing the same exact thing, except I get to watch both. Lay down; let her sit on your face." He moves to lie down on the ground, scoots her legs apart, and slides into position. He locks his arms around her legs, pulling her down. "Mmm, good boy."

"Mack, baby, I'm about to come," I pant out. "Please." Whatever he's doing down there to her, has Mar double timing on my cock.

He comes up for air long enough to get out, "Not until Mar does."

Fucker.

Mar starts sucking like she wants to win a state championship. I'm trying to pull her off, but she's not having it. I think Mack added a few fingers because she's grinding on his face even harder. "Come on, Mack. She's trying to make me come. The dirty talk in the video is making it even harder not to." I'm pleading here, but met with complete silence. They both love this shit.

I start with the last option I have… dirty talk. "Look at you, Mar, sucking my cock like the whore you are." I hear Mack groan, and she lets out the smallest whimper, slowing her sucking slightly. It's enough for me to hold off my orgasm, so I keep going, "You like being our little whore that we share, don't you? You love the power, but you love it even more being able to use that power while you're on your knees, milking an orgasm out of one of us. How bad do you want my cum?" I take a breath and then continue, "Trying to make me come with your mouth, while I'm watching you ride me on screen. All while I was drugged. And you're using my boyfriend's face right here in front of me."

Mack grabs his cock, squeezing it, pumping up and down at a punishing pace. With a quivering scream and our names on her tongue, Mar is the first to come.

I can get used to that.

Mack is right behind her, shooting his load all over his stomach and chest. That's enough to set me off, and I shove my cock further into Mar's throat as far as I can, grunting, "Swallow. Every. Last. Drop."

She pulls herself off me with a wild look in her eyes as she straddles my lap and taps the side of my face. I give her a weary look and part my lips as I let her spit my own cum into my mouth. Mack's on his knees, watching the show with the widest smile. He swipes two fingers through his own orgasm, gathering it on his fingers and shoving them into my mouth. Then he licks those same fingers with such a sweet-sounding hum.

Shrugging his shoulders and winking, he says, "Had to have all of us in there."

Satan… what did I do to deserve this?

* * *

We finished showering and took turns washing each other off. Aftercare is my favorite part, and I usually am the one who takes care of Mack, but I love that we're all taking care of each other—in our own ways.

We finished the video, and by the end of it, I was rock hard again. The shower didn't help that ache at all… both of them rubbing all over my body I figured my dick would never go back down. The last twenty-four hours have been a complete whirlwind in the best way possible. I hate to say it, but Mar fits right in with us, especially after all that happened last night. The amount of trust I have for this woman now is so indescribable.

They explained everything that happened after the filming was over as well. It warms my icy heart the way they did aftercare, even while I was knocked out. Especially when they fucked me into oblivion. That reminds me of that nagging question that's still yet to be answered. "Mar, what the fuck was that shit with Marcello last night?"

She half-ass answers me, "It wasn't anything."

"Bullshit. We won't be in whatever this situation is without knowing the full story," I command, waving my hands around. "Are you in danger? Does that now put us in danger? Marcello's a client of mine, but I wouldn't put anything past that man. He's dangerous and ruthless and always gets what he's owed. He'll end anything standing in his way. Lives included."

"I don't tell many people this, or really anyone, but I'm also tired of carrying all the burden on my shoulders." She sounds exhausted. "My father, Igor, runs the Russian Bratva here. As you're aware, I'm sure that after living in Vegas for longer than five minutes, Marcello Barone runs the Italian mafia here in Vegas. The Italian's run Vegas, meaning Barone is at the top. They all report to him in a sense. He gives them territory and certain things with which they can deal. Guns, specific drugs, brothels—you get the idea. It hasn't always been that way, though." She's staring off at the wall, seemingly stuck in a memory. "My father used to have all the power over the airport and the port manager. Any shipments coming into this city, he had a say over. Marcello's father ran their name into the dirt. Rumor has it that one of my dad's men killed Marcello's father. We don't know who really did it, but Marcello took over the Barone family when I was younger and knocked my dad out as headman in charge," she says with a nonchalant shrug, like any of this is normal shit to be talked about. "There's a ton of history; this was ten years ago at this point, but that sums up most of it."

"Wow. Okay, so why did he have you fired from Sins?" She flinches at my words. Fuck, she's still hurt over losing that job. "Why were you even working there if you're Miss Mafia Princess? Bratva Princess?" That was the wrong wording. Shit, she looks murderous right now.

"That's what I was trying to find out last night. Vincent, the owner of Sins, didn't give me a reason. And I'm not questioning that crazy fuck. He's even more unhinged than Marcello. That's his enforcer. Blood's on his hands constantly, and I don't want to be the next one that's getting tormented for fun. I'm glad I was just fired, and not some kind of therapy for his ass." She approaches me slowly, giving the impression that she wants to give me a kiss or do something sweet. But her hand swings up, gripping tightly around my neck.

Don't get hard. Don't get hard.

"Call me mafia princess again, and you won't see your next day." I give her a nod, and she releases me.

Mack chimes in, "My cocks hard… but I have more questions. Have you been in contact with your father?"

"I don't talk to that misogynistic piece of shit," she spits.

Okay, so that's a sore spot…

I hold my hands up in peace. "Hear me out. What if something has happened, or if your dad is making moves on the Italians? He could think you had something to do with it."

She cocks her head to the side, her brows pulling together. "How the fuck do you anything about the mafia?"

"I've seen plenty of movies." I shrug.

"He's lying. He loves mafia *romance* books," Mack throws out with a snicker. "Specifically, why choose, mafia books." He winks, and I swear my face has to be blood red.

I'm going to kill him—mafia style.

Mar is laughing so hard she lets out a snort. Now we're all laughing.

I'm just worried about her safety… from both sides.

I'm in my car, parked at my apartment complex, going over the last twenty-four hours. I'm already looking forward to seeing Mack and Percy again, and I shouldn't be… I don't catch feelings, and especially not this quick.

They are everything I've always dreamed of having in partners. In addition to being funny, responsible, and emotionally mature, they're drop-dead gorgeous!

Add the masks, plus they're already boyfriends…

Just start digging my grave.

But where does that put me? Their relationship with just the two of them is perfect as it is. Why would they need me coming in and crashing what they've already figured out?

Contemplating what I should do, I shoot off a text to one of my best girlfriends, Blair.

MAR

Finally made it home after a whirlwind twenty-four hours.

It's a Sunday. I don't think she's in the salon today, but then again, I don't know when she's not working. I feel like she's always there.

I'm walking up to my apartment as I throw my phone into my purse, but stop when I see a black chrome McLaren Speedtail pulled off on the side road. That's an expensive-ass car for this area of town. You see stupid, expensive sports cars on the strip all the time, but on the outskirts of town, not so much. I know it's not my father because even his dumbass wouldn't blow that much money on a car. I wouldn't have paid attention, but there's someone in it, and I can feel eyes on me, but I can't see through the dark tint. As I try to get a closer look, the car takes off wildly fast.

Opening the door to my apartment, I let out a sigh when my ass finally hits the couch. I know it was only one night, but my body is worn out. I couldn't imagine spending every day with them. A smile lands on my face, but I wipe it from my lips as fast as possible.

I cannot catch feelings for these two.

I shuffle through my purse looking for my phone to text Blair back. She lives in one of the other units in my apartment building. Being close in age, we've quickly become friends, and she's truly just a sweetheart. We all know each other in the building, but the other two tenants are little old ladies who bake sweet treats for us way too often. Then there are Blair and Ellie, who are roommates. I'm not as close with Ellie because she's constantly busy, but she seems sweet—like a black cat. Ellie and I are very similar in that way.

MAR

You at your place? It will be easier to explain in person.

The response is immediate, and now I'm not sure how I'm going to explain all the wild shit that has happened.

BLAIR

I'm coming over right now!

* * *

"We're past knocking?" I blurt out when I hear Blair come through the door. When I meet her eyes, nothing but pure excitement covering her face.

[1] *I'm fucked.*

She starts a mile a minute, "I was just texting you. Quit being dramatic and spill the beans. I was so fucking worried. It was bad enough that you went to their house the first time you met these random masked, thirst traps of men. Then you stay over there all night? Who are you, and what have you done with my man-hating Mar?"

She's the only one I told that I was meeting up with them. She knows I'm a cam girl, so that's going to make this a little easier to explain.

"So I got there, and they welcomed me in like a long-lost best friend. Mack is a literal sweetheart—the definition of a cinnamon roll. Percy was the one I was worried about. He's the more dominant one in their relationship, and I could tell he likes to have control over every situation, but

---

1. Girls Need Love (with Drake) - Remix - Summer Walker, Drake

he was perfectly welcoming. We shot some promo pictures for the live stream we're collaborating on next week. That led to them being on-screen messing around while I was off camera, telling them what to do." She looks at me, mouth agape, in shock. Then she starts smiling like the scheming brat she is.

She questions, "You like these two, don't you?"

Trying to blow off the serious question, I keep the juicy story going. "They made me come harder than I ever have." I shrug, not letting on that they're already working their way into my life.

I don't do relationships.

"That's a plus, but not what I asked." She's gone serious on me, which scares me more than anything. Blair is anything but serious.

"I think I do." Sighing, I throw myself back on the couch with a huff. "I don't catch feelings, though. I've known them for literally a day. There's no way… right?"

"If you know, you know," she says, looking off in the distance like she's somewhere else in her mind.

I practically whine, "They're dating each other." Mack said he wasn't on the monogamy train, so this is a waste of an excuse to bring up, but I'm reaching for anything at this point.

"I'm sure they would be open to it if they were fine with you joining in. Who wouldn't want you full time?" she huffs.

"I'm regretting telling you about this in the first place," I respond, trying to hide the smile on my face.

She commands, "No, you're not. You can't lie to me. Now spill, what else happened?"

"Well, we went to the new club, Club Onyx, and it was super nice, killer vibe, but then one of my dad's acquaintances, I guess is what you would call him, came up to us and kicked me out." Blair doesn't know anything about my father; sadly, I don't feel comfortable telling her. Not that I don't trust her, but I like keeping that side of me separate, and her not in danger. I was trying to get out of telling the boys, but they kept asking.

Blair looks confused, but I don't elaborate. She's gotten enough out of me for the day. "Huh, that's odd. Well, I'm pumped for this new business adventure you're on! Let me know if you need anything. Seriously, come by the salon so I can do your hair. You never let me." She's giving me those stern eyes that she doesn't pull out often.

"I will, I promise. Thank you for coming to check in on me," I assure her, and we stand up from the couch, hugging, as I walk her to the door.

I head back into my room to finally take a shower in my own bathroom. No matter how much the guys love their skincare, it's still not the same. I go through my every-thing, shower routine, washing my hair and body—sad to be washing them away.

I start to set up my camera. Why not stream? It's not like I have anything better to do. Getting into one of my lingerie pieces, I choose the all black and faux leather one. I always start off fully clothed. Well, I start off fully clothed, meaning my pussy and tits are covered. They're for sure paying money for me to strip out of anything. I have a couple of regular clients who pay me to do private sessions with them. Which is usually just me degrading them.

Pressing the button to start streaming, I'm finally live. Taking out some of my favorite toys, I position them on my bed in view of the camera. The clit stimulator, a molded dildo of one of my favorite porn star, and, of course, the OG wand. I still have so many other toys, but those are for playing with others. Well, besides my plugs, you can always use a good butt plug.

I usually sit for a few minutes after getting everything out, waiting for everyone to jump on, but they're really trickling in today. It's only been three minutes, and I'm already at my highest streaming number of guests that have joined… *ever*. I sit here in complete shock until a deep voice interrupts me from my thoughts.

Someone's in my apartment, and it's for sure not Blair.

@UNTRAINED_GHOSTT

MACK

W e were streaming when we got the notification that Mar was live. We told everyone in ours to head over to watch Mar, and they better treat her well. We're watching her get set up when suddenly, a deep voice booms through her apartment. She looks at the camera, and it looks like she's seen a ghost.

A real ghost, not me.

I look at Percy, worried, and he's wearing a matching expression, with a little more anger swirling around. "What do we do?"

He answers me in a rush, "I have no clue. We don't even know where she lives!" Percy's getting pissed, and I know it's because he has zero control over what's going on.

"I'm going to try to call her," I offer. Percy gives me a nod. I try calling her, but I shake my head as I hear her voicemail start. "Nothing… voicemail."

"Fuck!" Percy screams. He's going to lose it.

"Okay, okay, we can't freak out. Maybe it was just her dad," I try to reassure him.

"That might be worse than a random intruder," Percy

spits back. "It could very well be Marcello. He was pissed the fuck off last night!"

We know nothing about her real life, and this really opens my eyes to the fact that we need to dive a hell of a lot deeper than we have. That all takes time, and we don't have any, with her most likely in danger. Suddenly, I feel sick to my stomach.

Percy pulls his phone out, saying, "Let me try to call a couple of people from Sins. Maybe they'll give me something we can go off of. She could still have friends who work there."

It doesn't help a goddamn thing that all our social accounts are getting blown up with questions about Mar and if she's okay. I guess word got out that she abruptly ended her stream. We did send a ton of people over there…

* * *

We're in the living room trying to film for content, but our minds are elsewhere. I think Percy's about to snap someone's neck, and it'll most likely be mine with the specific TikTok we're trying to film. He called every contact he had for Sins, but they were all tight-lipped about anything involving Mar. He even asked about Marcello, but not a peep.

Obviously, I'm sure they value their lives.

For the video we're trying to film, "König" is positioned above "Ghost." So, he straddles my back and pulls my head up. Percy has his phone in his hand, and its screen faces the camera. He snaps the picture with his phone, then drops my head back down. It's trending right now, but it's not cosplayers doing it. Of course, Percy's marketing ass found the trend and has us doing it immediately.

This is our sixth take for this video, and Percy's huffing and puffing has me on edge. It's been off every time, so I question, "Can we take a break?" Any content we film for social media has to be up to Percy's perfection standards. Most of the time, it ends up with us at each other's throats. I usually love the content I film on my own. Normally, it's thirst traps or me shaking my ass with my gear on, or my fave… *air-humping*. They're hilarious to me, and they've grown my account the most.

"Sure, Baby Boy." He gives me a quick kiss after he rips off our headgear and masks, then pats my ass, sending me on my way.

Okay, I can't be mad at him now with the ass pats and the "Baby Boy."

I head into our room and pull the leftover blunt from last night out of my nightstand, and all that does is remind me of Mar, and a new wave of sadness washes over me. I really hope she's okay. We've absolutely blown her phone up today, but still no response.

Sparking the blunt up, I take a deep inhale. I'm spacing out for just a minute, thinking about how comfortable I instantly was with her. Taking a few more hits, I look up, and Percy's leaning against the door frame, holding himself up from the top with one of his arms.

Fuck, that's my weakness.

I lower my eyes and ask, "Is this how you ask me to get on my knees for you, because it's working?" His shirt and vest have ridden up, and his little patch of hair is peeking out, and it takes all my self-control not to groan.

He pushes himself off the door frame and walks over to me, looking like he really might eat me alive. "No, but that doesn't sound like a bad idea now that you mention it." He reaches out and plucks the blunt out of my fingers.

After taking a few hits himself, he puts it out in my favorite alien ashtray.

He's staring at me again, a heavy gaze that I'm already squirming under, wanting to dart my eyes away from his. He's still as worked up as I am from getting cut short earlier. We were going to finish fucking while watching Mar fuck herself, but that clearly didn't happen.

Before I can look away, he grabs my neck right under my jaw. His hand encloses my neck as he tilts my head up to keep my eyes on him. "Baby Boy, what have I told you about cowering away from me?"

I love it when he's like this with me.

He doesn't even give me time to answer that question. He crashes his lips against mine, and I hand over all the control as I give in to him. I call myself a switch, and don't get me wrong, bringing my dominant side out is fun every now and again. But I found my true happiness in submission. Taking orders and completely giving myself over to my partner is glorious. Throw some degrading in there, and I'm one happy man.

Percy pushes me back onto the bed to lie down. He stands up in front of me to his full six-foot-four height, and I let out a groan. "How did I get so lucky?" I ask while openly appreciating this specimen of a man.

He strips off all his gear, slowly, just for me. His swollen, leaking cock, swings between his legs. He exclaims, "Do you see what you do to me, Ghost? Why do you let those thoughts run through that pretty head of yours?" He doesn't even have to ask to see what kind of thoughts they were… he knows they were negative in some way. With concern lacing his features, he questions, "Is it from the shit we've done with Mar? We don't have to keep going if it makes you uncomfortable or if it makes you feel less than."

"No, it's not Mar or anything we've done the last few days. You know I get in my head sometimes. Occasionally, I have to fight with myself, thinking you're too good for me." I cower and look at the floor. "I sometimes feel like I ripped away the dream life you were on the path to having. That maybe I'm not good enough for you, and you could be with a woman, and that life could be yours."

I knew we were it, and I think he did, too, but the thought is always in the back of my mind—the guilt.

He grabs both sides of my face, knowing exactly what I need. "We're perfect for each other, Mack. I don't want you ever to doubt that I love you with every cell in my body. You're smart, breathtakingly beautiful, passionate, and so witty."

I give a shrug and try to look away, feeling tears wanting to drop. He loves me and my self-doubting mind better than anyone ever has, and I will forever be thankful for that. "I love you, Percy." I touch my forehead to his, and we sit there in a comfortable silence for a minute.

"Are you ready to be Daddy's whore now?" Nodding my head up and down like a damn bobblehead, I'm more than ready to get out of my head and into the subspace I crave.

He walks around to his side of the bed. I hear him rummaging through the nightstand, where he keeps all his toys and ropes. I don't dare look back at him, the suspense being my favorite. Feeling him climb onto the bed behind me, he grabs both of my wrists and pulls them to the center of my lower back. I haven't jumped into rigging like he has—I'm more of the rope-bunny type. He ties what feels like the red rope around each wrist several times. Once he lets go, I test it.

Yep. It's tight… just how I like it.

Hovering by my ear, he whispers, "What's your safe

word, Baby Boy?" He only checks that I remember it when he ties me up or we're doing a free-use scene.

I sigh, "Espionage." He lets out a deep chuckle. He came up with it, and again, I blame the mafia books.

He's on his knees behind me, his chest pressed to my back, and I'm trying to remember how long it's been since we've broken out the ropes. I've missed it, to be honest.

He starts to run his hands up and down my chest and stomach from over my shoulders, but I want to feel his hands on my skin. I'm not above begging for him to take these clothes and vest off of me. His dick's right where my hands are, and I can't control myself. I reach up and cup his cock and balls as he lets out a feral groan. Growling, he remarks, "Tied-up, greedy sluts don't get to touch, *remember?*" He runs a hand over my cock, barely applying any pressure. I shove my hips forward, seeking his hand.

"Please, Daddy." I'm still in my full gear. He hasn't taken anything off me yet, or allowed me to, and I know that's on purpose. He loves the fucking power play.

He pulls away from me, commanding, "Stand up and lean over the bed. Now!"

Scrambling off the bed, I do exactly as he says. He slowly climbs off the bed, completely bare in all his glory. He steps behind me, pressing up against my ass with his hips and hard cock. "Take your boots off." I toe each boot off with speed.

He reaches around me deathly slow, unhooks my belt, and pulls it out of the loops. Then he unbuttons my pants and pulls the zipper down. He drags them down my legs, freeing my cock, relieving some pressure from being pushed up against my cargo pants. My hands are still tied behind my back over my shirt and vest. I wish we were recording this so I could re-watch it from his angle. So I practically beg, "Daddy, can we record this?"

He tilts his head to the side before asking me, "The slut wants to put on a show?"

Yes. Yes. Yes.

Plus, there's no mask, so it'll be even better when we re-watch it. "Yes. I want to see all the angles you fill my holes. Leave the mask off. I want this just for us." He lets out a groan at my statement, then I feel him push off my ass, and he walks out the door.

Minutes later, he's setting up the tripod at the end of our bed. He stalks back to me, reaches around, palms me, and clicks his tongue. "You're leaking in your briefs like a needy whore." Letting out a whimper is all I can do at this point. I love being at the mercy of this man, and he gets to use my body any way he pleases.

Percy pulls my briefs down, finally freeing my dick. He reaches over me to grab something I can't see. I hear the lube top opening, and then I feel the cold metal pressing against my entrance.

He huffs out, "I have to get this tight hole ready while I shove my cock down your impatient throat." He works the plug inside my ass as he pulls the rope that secures my arms, trying to get me to stand. Then he turns me around in one swift motion, shoving both my shoulders down and pushing me to my knees.

He hums, "Mmm, right where you belong. Now open." He wastes no time tapping his cock on my tongue, then shoving to the back of my throat.

The plug comes to life, and I let out a gasp, which allows Percy to shove himself further into my throat. I'm a gagging, spitting, whimpering mess as he fucks into my mouth relentlessly.

My three favorite activities.

Grunting, he unexpectedly stops as he says, "Fuck, I'm

going to shoot down your throat if you keep that up. Stand up, Baby Boy."

I'm so hard, it hurts. "Daddy, pleasseee." He grabs my dick, stroking up and down two times, then releases it. I spin back around, and his hand is in the center of my back, bending me over the bed. Smacking my ass so hard it takes my breath away, the plug moves perfectly against my prostate. "More. Please." He starts raining down the smacks on each cheek. They sting, but the bliss that comes after is unmatched. At the sound of my whimpering, he stops to soothe each globe. I'm sure he's back there, admiring his handiwork from turning my ass red.

His voice is barely above a whisper, "Red's my favorite color on this creamy skin of yours." I rub my ass against him, begging for him to fuck me.

He unties me and climbs onto the bed. I look at him in confusion. "Wh—" He cuts me off.

"I want you to ride me, and you'll need your hands for this one. I want that cock bouncing just for the camera. I need you to watch this video back and appreciate this body of yours, and how well you take me."

I pull off my vest and compression shirt and breathlessly respond, "Please… I need you in me. Now." He pulls the lube out, pouring it straight on his dick, slicking it up while I straddle him. With my back to him, I stare into the camera, silently thanking Percy's design choices for putting the chest with the mirror above it, facing the bed.

Percy removes my plug nice and slow. I grab his cock, line it up, and take him to the hilt, letting out a loud grunt. This is exactly what I needed.

"Fuck, Mack, baby, slow down. I'm not going to last." The grip he has on my hips is punishing as he prevents me from slamming back down on him. He leans back against the headboard as I place my hands on his chest to hold myself up.

He stretches me so deliciously. I look back at the mirror, and all I see is my swollen cock bouncing up and down. Now I see why he wanted me in this position. "Daddy, make me come. Please," I beg, and I can't find it in myself to care.

He runs his hands up my back in appreciation, then slides them down, gripping my waist again. "My filthy whore wants to come? How should I do that?"

I'm still watching my every move in the mirror. "My cock, please. Touch it."

His hand slides from my hip, and he starts to stroke me way too fast. The way I'm slamming up and down on him… I'm not going to last.

"Come for me. Now," he growls into my neck, then bites down, sending me over the edge.

Turning around on his lap, I breathily say, "I love you so much, Percy."

He grabs both sides of my face, murmuring, "I love you too, Mack. Always."

* * *

I hear the shower starting as I wait for Percy to come and get me. He doesn't like it when I get up on my own after we have sex. He takes aftercare very seriously. But he comes running in, scaring the shit out of me, as he screams, "I found her apartment!"

"But we still don't know if she's there," I retort.

"Yes, but it's something. Let's shower real quick and head over there to see if she's home." This is the first sign of happiness I've seen cross his face since Mar's been missing.

We shower quicker than we ever have. Percy usually washes me from head to toe, but we both take care of ourselves, jumping out and drying off quickly. Throwing on some sweats and T-shirts, we head out the door.

Here's hoping Mar's at home for Percy's sanity. He's been trying to stay distracted all day, but I know he's trying to mask how much he already cares for her.

She previously said she didn't want commitment, but now she's got us both on our knees, ready to take any and every order.

"Well, well, well, look who's finally decided to wake up," the voice cackles through my hazy head.

Fuck… slowly opening my eyes, looking around, and they land on the bane of my existence.

Marcello fucking Barone.

Where am I, and how did this asshole get me here? Did he fucking drug me? He must have, because the last thing I remember was someone in my apartment. Doing a mental check over my body, but not feeling anything out of the ordinary, so it had to be a sedative.

He chuckles, "I was going to hack into Blair's phone and act like it was her texting you, but it seemed easier to grab you once I knew you lived in her building."

[1] I spit with rage, "How the fuck do you know, Blair?" He's not going to hurt her for something I'm sure my dumbass father has done.

"Oh, your BFF didn't tell you?" I give him the most

---

1. Dethrone - Bad Omens

unamused look I can muster. "That's my niece." He's howling with laughter, and I'm sure the look of complete shock on my face makes him realize that I don't know Blair like I thought I did. *Was that friendship all curated?* "We don't share the same last name, so that's always been easy to hide."

I look around, trying to figure out where I am, and it seems like he has me in a warehouse of some sort. My hands are zip-tied behind my back, and each of my legs is tied to a side of the wooden chair I'm sitting in. I only see Marcello, but I'm not dumb enough to think he doesn't have at least three goons outside guarding the place.

"Why the fuck am I here, Marcello?" I know how these little interrogations go, and I hate to tell him, but I've been no contact with my father for far too long to know what he's been up to.

I'm about to break that news to him when he starts talking. "Your slimy father is messing with someone very special to me." *Why does he sound like he has a heart right now?* "Igor has been a pain in my ass since I took over Vegas. I should've killed him then."

"And what the hell am I supposed to do about that?" I think he expected me to shut down after he told me he should have killed my father.

With a wicked smile, I shock him even more by saying, "You should have killed him. It would have saved me from a ton of pain and suffering at that man's hands. He's a vile human being."

"That's my plan, and I want you to take over and run the Bravata," he says casually, as if reading a grocery list.

Immediately, I yelp, "Excuse me?"

"You heard me. Don't play the dumb-bitch routine with me, Marfa. I know that your father trained you as soon as you could walk, and knowing him, he probably beat you for every mistake. It's not normal… and you know that." He's talking about me being a female and being trained like a son would've been. Most mafia leaders want boys so they can take over their empire. Mine didn't give a shit what I had between my legs, which was good but equally as bad at times. My father didn't want any more kids, and he sure as hell wasn't handing his precious empire over to a distant relative. He trained me in anything he could think of. Hand-to-hand combat, Jiu-Jitsu, guns, knives, how to manage the people under your reign, manipulation, the shipments of illegal products, you name it, I've seen it. It's a lot, and it was all drilled into my skull at a very, very young age. Never being able to talk about this shit with anyone was another added layer of trauma. Igor's boot camp from hell is what I always called it.

The boot camp was made for me and me only.

If I were a typical girl, I would've been the submissive virgin girl who listens to whatever anyone in power says to do—which was always men.

I'm gagging even thinking about it.

He knew I would've been killed by whoever I was married off to, and I wouldn't have been a good pawn. It still ended up bitting him in the ass, though. I never wanted the business, especially if he would still be around to complain about how I was running it.

He trained me well, and I finally got big enough and learned how to use being shorter to my advantage. He obviously got older, and I could hold my ground in the end. I was so fucking over it, though. I've removed myself so far from this world, and have never considered looking back... until this moment.

A few minutes pass as we stare at each other. I want

him to sweat my decision. I ask Marcello, "What does this entail?"

He starts to fill me in on his plan, "I'm going to kill your father within the next week. I really don't want you anywhere near it, but you need to be ready to go in and take over power. I need you on my side, meaning none of the guys under your father is taking over. You'll be given more territory and can work alongside me." I need to figure out how to get the territory and Russian businesses out of the depths of hell before he hands me more shit to handle.

I object to him, which most wouldn't dare do, but if Marcello wanted me dead, I would be already. "I don't need any more territory. I need you to take his little army out with him, and I *will* be there when this happens. I miss being in the chaos and busting heads, for old time's sake." I am out of practice, but it'll come back to me… hopefully.

He pacifies me by saying, "That's fine. You can have some of my men for the time being, and they can train your new recruits. I'll get Vincent to get in contact."

In my driest tone, I say, "Can you untie me now?"

He raises his brows in question. "You're not going to go ballistic again, are you? I had to dose your ass to get you here."

"You broke into my goddamn apartment while I was streaming. Pretty much naked, I might add. What the hell did you expect?" Okay, so maybe he was decent enough to dress me in a T-shirt and biker shorts before bringing me here, but still, fuck him.

"Quit with the dramatics. I was there to get a job done. I only have eyes for one woman." He rolls his eyes like the true drama queen he is, but also, he has me curious now.

Who is this poor woman who has caught his eye?

"We could have easily had a civil conversation in my

apartment, but no, you had to pull the damn theatrics out, didn't you? It's not a dick-measuring contest, Marcello."

"That mouth of yours is going to get you killed," he spits, annoyed.

I shrug and silently think—*yeah, it probably will.*

* * *

It's the middle of the night by the time Marcello has his driver drop me off at my apartment. Walking up the steps to my second-floor apartment, I let out a squeal. Percy and Mack are both asleep and leaning against my door.

What in the hell?!

How did they know where I live?!

I yell at them, "What the hell are you two doing?"

They shake themselves awake, looking at me like they've seen a ghost.

Mack pushes off the door, getting to his feet, wrapping his arms around me, whispering, "Oh, thank god you're okay."

I'll let that sky daddy "thank you" go this time.

"What are you talking about? Of course I'm fine." There's no way they know about the shit with Marcello.

"We were on your stream when we heard the deep voice, and you looked like you'd seen a ghost. Then the stream abruptly ended," Percy calls out from behind Mack, sounding like he was worried sick.

"Yeah… It was very random." Fuck, I'm going to have to tell them. This also explains why all the people were flooding into my stream.

I question, "How did you all know I was streaming?"

"We have notifications turned on for your profile. Duh?!" Mack exclaims, like I should know that answer already. There goes the unwanted stomach flips.

"We were streaming and got the notification, then we told everyone to head over to yours because that's where we were going. We sure as hell weren't missing your stream," Percy says so matter-of-factly.

"Well, thank you for sending everyone over. It was the highest number of viewers I had ever had. That is, until Marcello had to end it all." They both look at me with wide eyes and slack jaws. "I know you want to know what happened…"

Percy cuts me off. "Did he hurt you? He better not have touched a hair on your head." He picks up my arms and runs his hands all over my body, checking me for injury.

"Percy! Stop, I'm fine," I say, grabbing both his arms and holding them by his sides before I reach up to give him a kiss. It hasn't even been a day, and I was already missing their touch. "Come on, let's go in, and we can talk about what happened. The door had been unlocked the whole time."

"The suspense is killing me. Mar… Please tell us what happened. We were so scared." Mack is such a sweetheart. He sounds on the verge of tears, and it's slowly chipping away at my frozen heart.

[2] *My Luchik.*

"Ugh, I don't know where to start or how to make this sound sane to anyone not in this life." I shudder, just thinking about how I've immersed myself back into the world I tried so hard to separate from. I really thought I was done with it all. "My father, Igor, is a horrific man. I've known this my whole life, and he has done unspeakable things to me."

---

2. Ascensionism - Sleep Token

Percy grinds his jaw, his hands tightening into fists. "I'll kill him," he growls angrily.

Chucking, holding my hands up. "Woah there, smutty mafia man. Let me finish." I won't let him live down the fact that he reads spicy books. "Marcello could've easily had a civil conversation with me at his house, my apartment, or literally anywhere else. But he had to pull out the greatest theatrics known to man. He kidnapped me and told me he wanted to kill my father and then have me take over the Bravata." I finish with a shrug. They both stare at me, jaws on the floor for the second time tonight. "Did I finally find a way to shut you two up? Yeah? Perfect. Can we go shower and go to bed? I'm exhausted."

"Mar… Are you okay?" Mack's so worried, and Percy's still in shock.

"Yes, *Luchik*, my father is a disgusting human, and this is what he deserves. I know this is ludicrous to most people, but it's how it has to be. He's crossed one too many people, the most recent being Marcello. You don't survive crossing Marcello Barone."

"So, do we get to be mafia husbands?" I snort a laugh. Only Mack would ask that at this moment.

"I'm sure you don't want to be a part of this chaotic life—it's dangerous, *Luchik*."

They need to get out while they can.

[3] "You're stuck with us, Mar. You had us scared to death. I know you said you don't want anything serious, but hear us out. You fit perfectly with us," Percy starts.

"We felt like there was a piece missing, and you filled that void perfectly for the past twenty-four hours—blissfully, I might add. Then we thought you were hurt… neither of us could keep the feelings harbored away that

---

3. Never Know - Bad Omens

we have for you," Mack says, looking over at Percy with the softest eyes I've ever seen. "We want to be there alongside you—if you'll have us…"

I've felt the same way since leaving them yesterday, but I thought it was delusional to feel this, this early on… or it was just an obsession.

But all along, they've been feeling the same way I have.

"Can we talk about this more tomorrow when we're all not sleep-deprived and talking out of our asses?" I counter back. Mack's face falls, and I hope to Satan herself that I didn't just break this sweet boy's spirit.

FOURTEEN

Getting off the phone with Steve, I'm relieved to be taking a mental health day from work. I can't believe it's already Monday. I couldn't have possibly filled him in on all the shit that had gone on in the last forty-eight hours and stayed out of jail.

We all slept in Mar's king-sized bed, which was glorious. It truly made me realize how much I'm hoping Mar says she wants to see where this goes between us. Mack and I took up most of the bed with Mar in the middle; it was a pile of bodies and limbs, but it felt *right.*

We have some heavy shit to discuss about our future together when they both decide to wake up. Mack was upset last night when Mar wanted to wait until the morning, but I think it was the right plan. She needed time to decompress from everything that had happened this weekend before we started to pour our hearts out to her.

That would've had her running for the hills.

When we couldn't find her, it brought out the feelings I had been trying to bury deep inside me. I've never imagined myself being a part of any relationship besides a monogamous one. Honestly, I never knew it was a possibility until I met Mack. I always thought I was destined for the little white picket fence, the trophy wife, and the two-point-five kids.

I've been so happy with Mack, but Mar is the missing piece, and we had no clue we were missing it. Then she went and spilled all the shit about Marcello and his plans with her father… Where does that put us in that bizarre life? She's about to be head of the Russian Bravata… What caught me off guard was Marcello not even blinking an eye at Mar being a woman and wanting her to take over. It might be my new favorite thing about that unhinged man, and maybe, with them being partners in crime—literally—I could quit and work for him full time.

I mean, is that allowed? I need a mafia dos and don'ts handbook, pronto.

I know very little about this life besides what I've read, which I know is fiction… but there has to be some truth behind them, right?

Mack just had to blab his gums about it. She's never going to let me live that down.

We would blindly support her in any life; she just needs to accept us into hers. I know it's a dangerous world to live in, especially as the leader of a family. You automatically have a target on your head, along with anyone you associate with.

I hear movement in her bedroom. I walk in to see Mack's head in between Mar's thighs. "Goddamn, have you two even brushed your teeth yet?" I blurt out, trying to hide a chuckle. Mar's eyes slowly blink open, and she gives me a sleepy smile.

"Yes, old man. There's an extra toothbrush under the sink. Go, and then come join us." She shoots me a wink that heads straight to my cock.

I don't know why it's so thoughtless for me to follow her commands, but it feels good not having to worry about shit for once. I'm in charge of so much daily—it feels good not to be for once.

Walking out of the bathroom, Mack's still in between her thighs, and her head is thrown back in bliss. He sucks her clit into his mouth, fingers pumping in and out of her. "Keep going, Mack; I'm almost there!" She lets out a scream, squeezing her thighs around his head. "Fuck, *Luchhiikk.*"

She is so goddamn perfect when she comes. That thick body of hers convulsing and Mack's glorious frame in between her thighs—it's a sight to see. I shout out to them while she's in her post-orgasm bliss, "I was going to say we could do our debut stream, but I just remembered we don't have our masks with us."

"Ma'am, or should I say Mommy? Can you bring your toys to the house?" Mack chuckles. The "mommy" sends the breeding kink into overdrive.

She lifts her head, and asks Mack, "Does the whore want to be pegged?"

Fuck, she's unhinged.

He bobs his head, and she's up and out of bed before I blink.

"We need to have a talk before we get to the fun, Mar," I say, wincing internally at the look in her eyes. "We don't want to keep these feelings locked up."

"Percy, I know you like to plan everything in your life, but have you ever thought about having fun for once?" She's not getting rid of us, so I'll take that as a maybe. "I want to see where this goes. Damn, do I need to spell it out for you?"

Mack is smiling as if he's won the lottery. "Yes! I knew

you wouldn't be able to resist us together. Masked up and ready to take any command you throw at us."

He's going to be the one to scare her off. I'm sure of it.

* * *

We make it back to our place after grabbing some takeout on the way there. We eat and chit-chat like this is a normal thing we do together.

Maybe it can be from now on.

Mar packed an "overnight bag." Well, more like three of them—and they're huge. I'm pretty sure one whole bag was full of only sex toys.

Not that I'm complaining.

Hopefully, she decides to stay with us for a little while. I don't like that Marcello could get into her apartment so easily. I'm sure he has some high-tech hacker who can do his dirty work, but I still like knowing I can keep her safe with us in the same place.

We posted on our socials today, telling our followers we were having Mar over to do our first stream together. They're all foaming at the mouth over this, but to say I'm nervous would be the understatement of the year.

Mack and I are getting ready in our room while Mar is freshening up in our ensuite. We all just got out of the shower, and I really don't know how we kept our hands off one another.

I slide my pants over my hips, loop my belt through, and then strap my leg holster over my upper thigh. The placement is a science, and I look up just as Mack throws his identical leg holster in place.

Mar opens the door, and I let out a groan while Mack starts whistling and catcalling her from across the room. I compliment her, "Fuck, you look you're ready to take charge."

"That's the plan, boys. Now, let's go. I have some big plans for tonight," she says.

I don't know what scares me more: streaming for the first time with her or finding out what she has planned for us. She is wearing a red leather lingerie outfit. The corset bodice accentuates the halter-style top, which exposes her beautiful breasts with cutouts in the leather. She completes the look with a matching leather thong and fishnet stockings, connected by a contraption around her waist.

All I want to know is how she got into this on her own.

I'm about to ask when she snaps us into motion. "Are you two going to keep ogling, or are we going to get this show on the road? This leather thong is about as comfortable as you can imagine."

I look toward Mack, his dick straining behind his pants, matching mine. We're beyond fucked when it comes to this woman. We place both our masks on and walk into the living room. Mar's dragging her huge bag filled with her toys behind her.

Mack's quick to set up the camera on the side of the couch, while I get the front one going. Mar stands aside, watching us work. "I feel like I should learn to set up, but when I have two masked men to do it, why should I?" she says, flopping dramatically onto one of the accent chairs she loves.

I ask, "Are you both ready?" They each nod, and I hit the stream button. The chat is already popping off as Mar rummages through her bag.

$250- BEMYMOMMY

Where's @Devils_sovereign? I've been waiting since y'all announced it. I was not about to miss this!

She has two prostate massagers out, as she answers the chat, "I'm right here. Had to get my toys out for tonight."

One for each of us, and goddamn, those are thick. They have cock rings around them as well.

I read the next chat out loud:

$38-KÖNIGSCUMDUMPSTER

Mommy, is that you? Let Daddy König fuck you tonight!

I grunt, "They have the right idea. I can't wait to get in that tight cunt again."

Mack takes my previous thought about Mar's collection right out of my head. "I think you keep the sex stores open. What else is in that goodie bag?"

He walks toward her and the bag, and when she stops him, she commands both of us, "Nope, out of those clothes. Both of you get on the couch beside each other. Knees to chest. I'm going to get these in you. I have plans for your holes, and I need them ready." We follow her instructions, and she jokes, "Who even goes to physical stores for sex toys anymore, Ghost? I think I might turn the old-man jokes your way instead."

She pulls out a dildo-looking thing, sets it on the chair, and walks over with the massagers. The dildo has another hook on the opposite end.

Very interesting—that bag really is never-ending.

"Read the chats. I don't want them piling up," she says, rolling her eyes. "I want them to hear how needy these toys make my little fuckdolls."

I read the chat out loud because the next screen name is hilarious:

$57- PUSSYSLAYER9000

I want to be your fuckdoll, Sovereign!!!

Mack and I are in position, so I ask Mar, "You like what you see, Mama?"

She lets out a satisfied hum, but is quick to let everyone know who's in charge. "Did I ask the fucktoy to talk?" My cock fliches on my stomach—the degradation spurring me on. She takes the massagers in her hands and starts to lube them up. "Ghost, read a chat. Pick a good one."

$200- FÜCKMEAT

I'm manifesting some pegging from the domme mommy.

"A man can only hope she brought a pegging device," Mack responds breathlessly, looking up at her.

[1] She pushes the prostate massagers into both of us at the same time, then purrs, "I need my filthy whores to be nice and relaxed. Breathe König, or you'll make this a lot harder than it needs to be. Fuck, I wish we could drug your ass again." The chat's going berserk. "And yes, we filmed that for you greedy cunts. It will cost a pretty penny and come with plenty of trigger warnings. We used this tight little body like the worthless rag doll he is." My cock is so fucking hard, it's embarassing. That mouth on her is downright sinful. "Look at you both. Already leaking all over yourselves. *Pathetic.*"

Mack lets out a whimper. I don't know who likes the degrading more at this point, me or him. "Ma'am, please."

"Please what, Ghost?" she taunts, with a menacing look. "I have lots of plans for tonight, and my back hole needs prepping, too."

I'm up and behind her before she can say anything else. Whispering, "Let me." I push her shoulders down on the couch. She taps Mack's thighs, and he scoots up, sitting

---

1. Into It - Chase Atlantic

with his legs sprawled out. She makes her way between them, taking his pulsing cock into her mouth. I spread her ass cheeks apart, carefully lifting my mask halfway up my face, and dive in, lapping at her back hole. Her breath hitches when I shove my tongue inside. I reach behind me where she has what I'm guessing is the anal plug for her ass.

Sliding my hand around her hip and down her stomach, I find her clit, and pinch it between my fingers. I murmur, "This tight cunt's already dripping for us, Mama." That has her pushing against my face. I don't know if it's to shut me the fuck up or if she loves the dirty talk.

I'll go with the latter.

Mack gasps, "I love when you eat my ass, Daddy, but you look so good devouring Sovereign's." Pulling my mask back down, taking the lubed-up plug, and pushing it against her back hole.

"Has anyone been here?" I ask.

"What do you think, *Papochka*?" she spits in the most condescending tone.

"I just wanted to know how easy I needed to be, but now, I'm showing no mercy." I finish pushing the plug into her, rubbing a couple more circles around her clit. Kneeling behind her, I run my cock up and down her slit. "Can I, Mama?" She doesn't even answer; as it lines up with her entrance, she pushes back onto me. "Fuucckkk. This cunt's made for us." She continues bobbing up and down on Mack's cock. I'm surprised he's still holding it together.

Right as I start pumping in and out of her, the prostate massagers come to life via a little remote Mar's holding. Mack lets out a gasp. Holy shit, this feels good.

She demands, "Read the chat, Ghost, and no coming,

neither of you. I want the cum in me. Both holes—dripping."

Mar only gets a couple more sucks in before Mack pulls her mouth off him. "Ma'am, please stop talking. Or I'm going to come down your throat."

"Read, Ghost!"

Oh shit, she's not playing anymore.

$21- @KÖNIGSGIRL444

I'm subscribing on every platform if this is what we're going to be getting. I've never seen anything hotter. 😭

He's still reading as Mar gets up and positions him to lie down on the couch horizontally. She shoves the bottom half of his mask up and straddles his face.

I stand back watching them with the massager still rubbing my prostate, wondering how she's going to keep us going. Everything already feels so good. The cock ring is still wrapped tight around both of our cocks, making them painfully hard to the point they're almost purple from all the blood pulsing to them.

"Fuck me from the back again, König. Your boyfriend's going to eat me while your balls slap him in the face."

How in the fuck does she come up with this?

I have no clue… but I'm sure as hell not going to question her ways.

Sinking back into her pussy feels like I'm coming home from a long vacation. I grit out, "This cunt was made for me, Mama."

Smacking her ass a little harder than I expected. She lets out a feral moan in response.

Fuck yes, she likes to be spanked.

I'm slamming into her while my groin is hitting the plug in her ass. She grinds down on Mack's face, and that has my dick rubing her G-spot. Mack plays with my balls and moves his hand back toward my taint. He starts probing, trying to find my prostate from the outside.

I'm really not going to be able to last.

I need her to come, now! I'm instructing Mack, "Suck hard, Baby Boy." Gripping the plug between my fingers and fucking her in and out with it. She starts mumbling and moaning, not able to form any words, lost in her pleasure. She throws her head back in pure bliss, enjoying everything being given to her. Mack has her legs pinned and gives her one final suck, causing her to scream, "Ghost, König, fuucckkkk." We can hear the chat in the background… It's out of control, and we're nowhere near done.

"You're beautiful when you come for us, Ma'am," Mack says, while running his hands up and down her thighs as she comes down from her high.

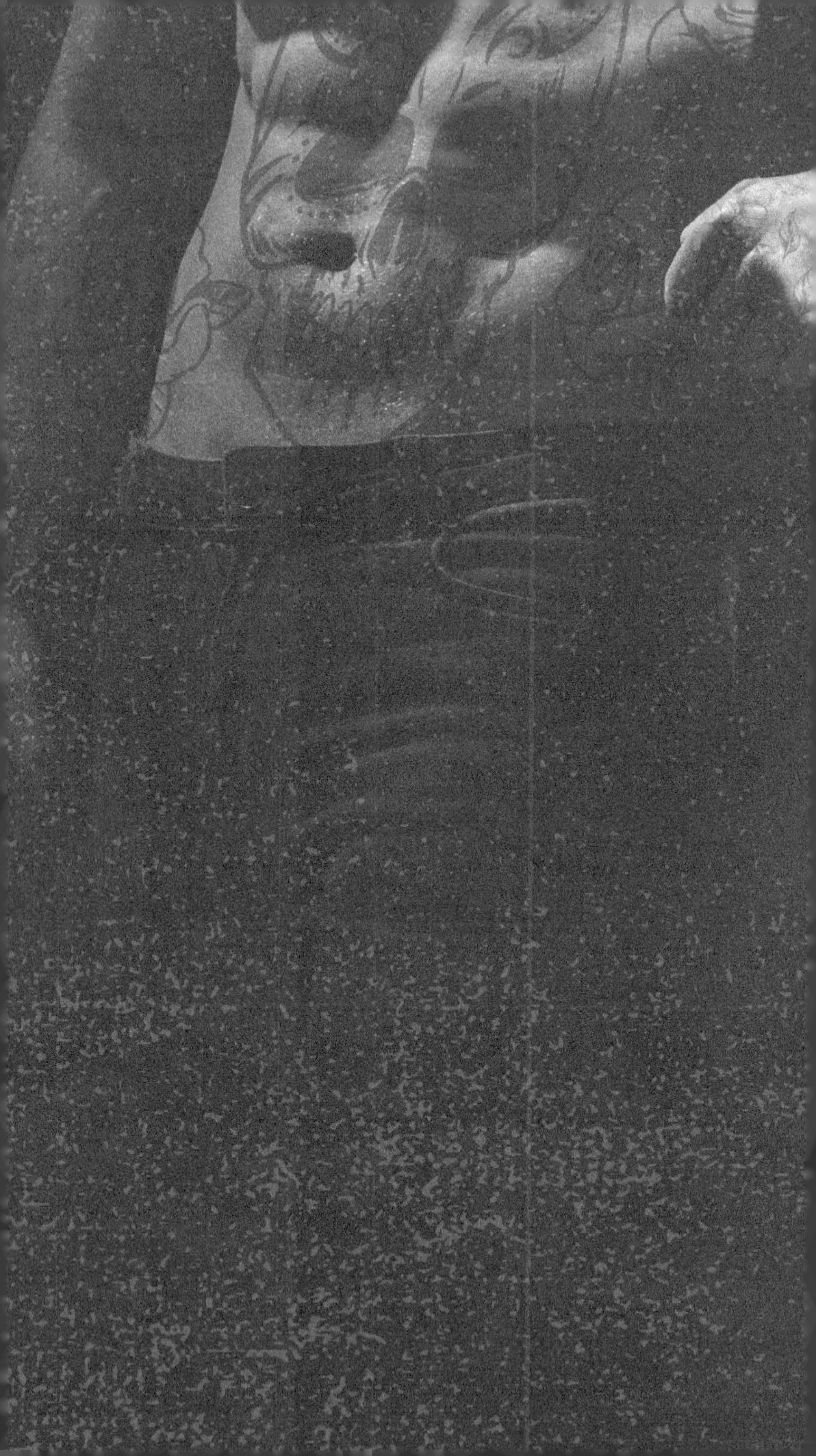

I pull my mask back into place, ensuring the subscribers don't see more than they already do. Running my hands up and down Mar's thighs, I move to squeeze her perfect tits. "Mmm, I love these."

"Okay, out König." She shoves Percy away so she can stand, hopping off of my face. I'm excited to see what she has up her sleeve now. "You ready to be pegged like the little whore you are? König and I are going to take you to Paris, *Luchik*." She runs her hand down the side of my face, and I lean into her touch.

I chuckle and shurg. "I've always wanted to go to Paris."

She makes her way to the accent chair, grabbing what looks to be a dildo, but it has another hook attached to it. She holds it up to the camera, showing it off to our subscribers. "What? Did you all think I was going to be strapping up?" She continues waving the toy around in front of the camera with a mischievous smile. "Nope, it's my favorite strapless strap-on. It even has a vibrator for my clit. I hope that hole of yours is ready for me, *Luchik*."

[1] Percy holds my legs up and starts fucking me with my plug, getting me nice and ready for Mar. Moaning, I whisper, "Keep going, Daddy. Please, that feels so good."

Percy barks his orders, "Up on your hands and knees. Move that ass toward the side camera; let the subs see the plug in your slutty, stretched hole." Complying, I get to my hands and knees and move the way he wants me. I quickly glance over at Mar and see that she's inserting the hooked end of the toy into her pussy.

Interesting.

Oh shit, now she's pushing a bigger plug inside her ass. She steps up beside me to see the view of my stretched hole, telling Percy, "König, hold his cheeks open. I want to see this ass gape." My chest hits the couch as I turn my head toward the TV screen and see the chats pouring in. Fuck, we're at an all-time high of active viewers, but I can't even focus on that right now.

Mar pulls my plug out nice and slow. "Look at that selfish hole, wanting it back inside." She pulls my cheeks even further than Percy already has them. My hole is surely gaping now, and I can see it as clear as day on the screen. She takes the lube and rubs it on the dildo connected to her. Percy finally lets go of my ass, but not before he gives me a sharp slap. A loud gasp leaves my mouth before I can stop it, followed by a small whimpering moan.

I love it when he gets rough with me.

Mar lines up behind me, teasing my hole as she says, "Fuck, look at my slutty, little masked whores. No coming still… there's just one more thing I want to try after this."

I feel the dildo sliding against my hole, and as I start to push back, she slaps my ass in return. "Quit being a needy

---

1. You - Jacquees

whore." I whimper at her words. She pushes inside me and turns the vibration on for the toy. The toy hits her G-spot, and the bullet vibrator plays with her clit just right. The sensation of the pulse while being fucked with the toy is almost too much. It's definitely not as thick as Percy's cock, but it's still a lot.

Percy positions his cock in front of me, shoving into my mouth before I can say anything to Mar about the dildo. I attempt to look to the side to see myself being spit-roasted on the TV. "The whore wants to see himself?" Percy questions with a sultry voice. I bob my head up and down in answer. He scoots over a hair so I can turn my head, and still keep his cock in my mouth. I groan at the glorious sight before me.

Mar instructs. "Read your chats, König." Her tits are bouncing up and down, accentuated by her corset top, and they've never looked better. I want to reach down to my cock, but I know I'll be coming in seconds, and I have to hold off. This is by far the most intense edging I've ever experienced.

Percy starts to read the chat aloud:

$57- @WHOREISH.DEVIL

Sovereign, you look so sexy fucking Ghost's ass!

"I know, babe, thank you. Love the username, by the way," Mar answers the subscriber like she's not pounding into me so fucking hard.

Percy keeps going, giving the subs what they want.

$17- @FILLALLMYHOLES

I want Ghost's lips around my fat cock!

Mar sputters, "I bet big money they have a micropenis." I'm choking on a laugh. She truly has no filter.

I'm dancing on the edge of release as the silicone cock hits the spot deep inside me. Pulling away from Percy's cock I whine, "I need to come. Please let me come, Ma'aaammm."

I don't care if I sound pathetic.

"No." One word. *Fuck!* She's set the perfect pace and pressure against my prostate to keep me right there, but never gives me more to push me over.

She pumps in and out a few more times, giving me one last hard smack to my ass and pulls out fast. I whimper in protest as she leaves me feeling empty. Percy pulls out of my mouth and lowers my mask back into place.

"That hungry hole is going to be filled again—hold on. Both of you lie on the couch. Each on one end. I want you so close that your asses and balls are touching." Neither of us move, looking at her like she's officially lost it. We snap into action immediately when she breaks our silence by clapping.

We move to get into position as she turns back to her bag of never-ending fucktoys.

We maneuver our legs so that our bodies are close enough to touch each other. Looking up, I see Mar devilishly grinning as she holds a goddamn double-sided dildo up.

Oh, this is going to get good.

"Are my toys nice and ready? And not you," she says to the fucking dildo. "You two fucktoys." That's all I ever want to be.

Her fucktoy.

She lubes up each end and goes to put one side into me first. Percy still has his massager and cock ring on, so she slides the cock ring off of Percy's dick and then pulls the massager out, immediately pushing the other end of the double-sided dildo into him. This is already so much, and I know she has something else planned.

She reaches down, pumping the dildo between us before hitting a button that causes the toy to come to life. The vibrations elicit a gasp from us both—like we need more vibrating stimulation.

"Okay, I'm coming up now. Percy, you get my ass." She starts to fist his cock, pumping up and down. He hisses at her tough grip. "I want this thing to stretch me until I scream." She reaches behind her, pulls her plug out, and throws it on the floor. Percy grabs the lube and pours some onto the hand Mar has around him. Climbing up on top of us, she positions herself facing me. With her legs on each side of my stomach, she's at an angle to receive both of our cocks.

I groan and say, "Can you come just from the sight of the prettiest pussy you've ever seen?" She takes the lube that's left over on her hand and runs it up and down my length.

"I don't know, but you better not test it out right now," she answers.

"Mama, I don't know how long I'm going to last," Percy grits out like he's in pain. She lines her pretty pussy up to my cock and slams down on it. Bouncing up and down a few times, her tits move in perfect rhythm. I throw my head back with the most roaring, animalistic moan I've ever heard.

"You feel like hea—" I stop mid-word, careful not to mention god or heaven. "Hell," I grind out. She gives me a grin like she knows she's trained me to a T. The sound of chats coming in plays a steady soundtrack in the background.

That's the last thing I'm worried about at this moment.

The only thing my mind comprehends is Percy

coaching Mar on how to fit his dick inside her ass. "Relax, Mama, let me in. I need to feel my boyfriend's cock on the other side of your walls. We're going to fill you so perfectly." She slowly—oh so slowly—sinks onto both of our cocks. She's a moaning and whimpering mess. "You're so tight… Too fucking tight." His arms shoot up to her hips to hold her in place. "Hold on, I can't come yet, fuucck-kkk." Then he thrusts a couple of times to get his bearings and groans, "This juicy ass right in front of my face as it's swallowing up my cock. You were made for us, Sovereign."

"Fuck, I'm so full," Mar moans out.

I grit out through a clenched jaw, "Fuck, shut up, both of you; I'm going to come from just your filthy words." Mar sets a punishing rhythm, bouncing up and down on our cocks. While Percy and I continue to grind back and forth as much as we can on the double-sided dildo, I reach up and press a firm thumb to her swollen clit. "Mmm, look at that greedy cunt devouring my cock." I turn my head to look at the screen. "Your ass looks so good with my boyfriend's fat cock in it."

I try to distract myself from Mar on top, taking both of us so well. She's everything I've ever dreamed of. Getting to fuck her while my boyfriend does the same is the ultimate dream. I really can feel him inside her, with just a thin piece of her skin separating us.

"What do we think, Devils? Are they ready to come?" Mar questions the subs, and I've never manifested harder for a "yes."

$500- @SPANKMEMOMMY

Please let them come, Mommy. Can they clean you up after?

"Fuck for $500, I'll tell them to do anything." She barks out a laugh. She starts violently moving on top of us, and I pick up the speed of my thumb on her throbbing clit. "I'm about to come, fuck, I'm about to co—" She's squeezing me so tight, and I let go right as she screams our names.

Well, our screen names.

Percy is right there with us. As we all reach the release we've been desperately waiting for, our combined moans and screams fill the room.

He scoots up the couch, slowly pulling the dildo out of his ass and repeating the steps on me. Mar goes to lie down on the couch, looking straight at Percy. "You heard the Devils. Clean me up, *Papochka*."

Percy's more than happy to oblige. "More than happy to. Can't wait to suck my boyfriend's release from this pretty cunt of yours."

"Shit, you two… I seriously cannot get hard again," I say, flopping back on the couch but still paying attention to them being hot as fuck.

"Mmm, you taste so good together," Percy moans as he leans up to give Mar a heated kiss. "Excellent, isn't it?" She gives him a nod, looking dazed.

"How are we ever going to top that?" I question. They shrug, and Percy reaches for the laptop, closing the stream. He's got everything he could ever want right here with us.

A YEAR LATER...

"Mack, I swear to fuck, if you put one more Pinterest board in my face, I'll call Marcello, get his jet, and we'll be on a flight to elope in Bora Bora tomorrow." [1] His whole face lights up, and I instantly know I've fucked up. He came barreling into my office with another sixty pins to look at for the wedding he thinks we are having. Mack and Percy both got down on one knee exactly six months after that first night we all spent together, and Mack has been planning every detail since.

He gets his phone out, putting it up to his ear. "Marcello! Buddy, how ar—" He pauses. "Got it, no buddy… well, big favor then. Mar just threatened me with your jet and eloping in Bora Bora, and I was just thinking about

---

1. No Need for Introductions, I've Read About Girls Like You On The Backs of Toilet Doors - Bring Me The Horizon

how perfect that would be, especially with how hard she's been working."

I start to bark out a threat, "Ma—" but he cuts me off, throwing his hand up in my face, not even looking at me. I grab his balls through his short athletic shorts, and he lets out a squeak, causing him to look at me finally. I take my thumb, running it across my neck, telling him to abort mission while still holding on tight to his balls.

He keeps talking away, "Next week? Yes, that's perfect. You know Percy will be out of the office, too, right?"

Percy's been working for Marcello—and Marcello only —since I've taken over as head of the Bravata, and Percy's loving every minute of it. He's finally got Marcello's marketing straightened out with all his businesses, so it really would be the perfect time to take the much-needed vacation we all deserve.

It's almost been a year since I started running my empire, and I don't have much to complain about. It's been tough finding men to train and trust, but Vincent, Marcello's second, has been helping me with that.

I found my second, Natalia Morozov—she's about as much of a badass as me. I knew I wanted another female as my second because there are already too many cocks in power in this world. It's been fun teaching her the ropes, and it's even more fun seeing our enemies laugh at the sight of two women coming for them; that is, until they're hanging from their ankles in one of Marcello's torture rooms. She's found her favorite specialty room in the warehouse and thoroughly enjoys getting to prove how effective she is in said room.

Mack pockets his phone and spins toward me, filling me in on the plans. "We're leaving this Sunday and spending a week in Bora Bora. I'll call my vacation planner when I leave here. Marcello did say we needed to take Vincent with us for protection."

I huff, "Protection?"

"Yes, Sovereign, please don't fight with him on this. You know what's going on right now in your world." I roll my eyes at him, but I'm not fighting about it. The Albanians have started an all-out war with us and have brought all of their syndicates together to come after us. It's been one thing after another, and I would be lying through my teeth if I said I didn't need a break.

What's better than a week at the beach getting railed by my soon-to-be-husbands?

"I'm bringing Blair then, too," I sigh to Mack as he approaches my desk. My one goal this trip—well, besides getting married—is to get Vin and Blair together. I have a suspicion they've been fucking around. And I know he doesn't want to step on Marcello's toes since Blair is Marcello's niece, but that girl has been down bad for him since I met her. And I see the way Vin looks at her.

Call me Match makin' Mar, I'm making this shit happen.

He raises his eyebrows at me, likely knowing precisely what I'm scheming up. "Let me in on the plan, Sovereign!"

"No, you don't know how to keep your mouth shut. I have to gag you in order to keep any secrets," I say with a wicked smile on my lips. Gags are my favorite to use with these two, but I have a special order coming in specifically for Mack. What better place than our honeymoon to break it in?

"Fine. It'll just be a surprise for me, too." With that, he kisses my lips and is out my office door, likely heading to his shop to check up on everything there.

* * *

I twist the key to lock my office before going directly to the door that joins Percy's office to mine. I bought the whole building to lease office spaces as a way to funnel my illegal money through a legal business. I knock on Percy's door, then hear him call me in.

[2] I sit down in the chair in front of him, throwing my legs up on his oversized desk and testing the water to find out what he knows. "Have you talked to your boyfriend today?"

"No, he's been ignoring me since I texted him asking why Marcello blocked off all of next week in my calendar." I smile wickedly at him, but he continues, too immersed in whatever he's doing on his computer screen with his black square-frame glasses on. "The only thing it says is, 'per Mar and Mack, you're taking off' at the top of the email." He huffs and lies back in his chair, hands steepled across his stomach, then he finally looks at me.

"We're all off next week… We'll be in Bora Bora." I wait for the gasp or the shit ton of questions that I'm sure Mr. Type A himself has—but they don't come.

Instead, he says, "Thank fuck! I need a break away from this shit." The bags under his eyes are the sure sign he needs a break, but I know he truly loves his work.

I get up and walk around his desk, scooting up on top of it. He has the perfect view of my bare pussy under my leather skirt as I place my feet on the armrest of his chair. I question him as I rake my eyes up and down his body, "You're not going to ask what we're going for?"

He scoots up as close as he can get to me, running his hands up my thighs, questioning, "What are we going for, Mar? I'm guessing vacation."

I shake my head, looking down at him in his dress

---

2. Break from Toronto - PARTYNEXTDOOR

pants, which are now sporting a massive erection, and his white button-up shirt, the top three buttons left wide open. "Nope. We're going to elope and have our honeymoon. Also, a much-needed week away from this hell-hole of a city." This city really isn't a hell hole; it's more so the people in it that won't leave us the fuck alone and stop causing shit.

Percy takes his pointer and middle finger and runs them through my folds. "You like what you see, *Papochka?*"

He groans a response, bordering on a growl, "This is proof enough." He moves his free hand down to his cock, groping it, showing me exactly what I do to him.

I shrug, dragging my booted foot down his stomach all the way to his groin, purring my response, "How about we FaceTime our boy toy and get him riled up?" He's already pulling his phone out and propping it on the bookshelf behind his desk.

He clears his desk of all its contents by pushing them clean off. Grabbing both of my shoulders, he lays me flat on his desk. My legs spread out, leaving me completely bare to his eyes and apparently Mack's as well. "Well, well, well... what do we have here?" I hear Mack's voice echoing through the phone's speaker, but I don't pay any mind to it as Percy's hand lands between my thighs.

He takes a seat nonchalantly beside me, pushing my leg up even further, then he has both hands on each side of my pussy, spreading me wide. "Look at our wife's pretty pussy, Baby Boy."

"I'm not your wi—"

Smack.

This motherfucker just slapped my pussy.

And why did I like it?

Percy growls out, "You're about to be," as he starts to rub my clit in tight circles with his two fingers. I look up at the phone to see Mack has his propped up, his cock is in his hand, and he's thoroughly entertained.

These two are going to be the death of me.

"No coming, Mack. And you're not getting to yet either," Percy barks out as he stands up, adjusting his massive cock within his pants.

"Excuse me. I'll just do it myself." I reach down, hand over my cunt, raising my eyebrows in contest, telling him to try me.

"You'll both wait until we get home." I know this is punishment for keeping our little secret from him, but we wanted it to be a surprise. He's so similar to me in the way he always has to be in control, so Mack and I are never really able to surprise him. Marcello just had to go and blow it.

I'll give him the power this time, but not without some annoyance first. "Okay, Big Daddy."

As we step onto Marcello's private jet, I have to remind myself not to drool as my jaw hangs wide the fuck open. [1] I was thinking the plane was going to be on the smaller side, but no. This goddamn plane is bigger than some commercial ones I've been on.

I'm truly scared to know how much it's worth.

Last night, I edged these two while live-streaming, and to say I was in my element is the biggest understatement. We don't get to stream as much as any of us would like to now, but it was nice being back at it last night. The subs were eating out of the palms of our hands.

As we walk further into the cabin, Mar introduces us to the flight crew while my eyes take in the plane's interior. It looks like an average living space with fancy leather seats spread throughout. The blonde flight attendant speaks up, "There's a full bathroom in the bedroom at the back of the plane. Also, there is another bathroom up by the cockpit door. Dinner will be served in a couple of hours. The full

---

1. Planez - Jeremih, J. Cole

bar is available per Mr. Barone, and we are here for anything else you may need."

Mack butts in, "Did she just say bedroom?!" Mar's head spins around so quick, piercing Mack with a look that could kill. He's been on thin ice the last couple of days… annoying the shit out of her with all the wedding plans he has. This was supposed to stop all the planning and stress because we are just eloping. But Mack called the resort and has been feverishly planning what seems like it's going to be a whole-ass wedding since he got off the phone with Marcello last week.

I reach up, smacking Mack's ass. "Leave the questions for later, Baby. We have a long flight. You can ask all the questions once we're in the air." The thought of putting that bedroom to use has my cock thickening way too fast. Add in the flight crew, and Blair and Vin being able to hear… Go ahead and make me captain of the mile-high club. This could be a once-in-a-lifetime chance.

I'm sure as fuck not missing it.

We get seated for takeoff. The pilot comes out to introduce himself, and he lets us know that we'll be in the air for over fourteen hours. I'm not the biggest fan of flying, but I figured a private jet would be better, and from the sound of it, it's going to be.

Before I know it, we've been in the air for over an hour, and I'm down one scotch.

A very fancy scotch, I might add.

I peek over at Blair and Vincent, and she's passed the hell out on his shoulder. He's nose-deep in his laptop, likely working on something for Sin's. Mar mentioned something about scheming up a plan to get them together finally… and my only instruction was not to share the scheme with Mack. He's not the best with secrets.

I eyes land on Mack, and my lips pull into an appreciative smile.

"What are you smiling at, Daddy?" Mack purrs, raising his brow in question.

I chuckle while filling him in on what was going through my head, "Just that you can't keep a secret to save your life."

"Hold on! What do you know that I don't?!" he pleads.

Mar grabs the back of his neck, massaging and running her hand up the back of his skull, and any thought that was in that head of his is gone in pure bliss. "Nothing, *Luchik*. Now, if you keep being good, I might take you two back to that bedroom and put it to good use."

The smirk covering her face says we're sure as hell going back there. I look over at Vin to see if he heard all of that, and he raises his brows but gives me nothing else to go on. He has to be fine with a bit of voyeurism, right? He owns a goddamn sex club, for fucks sake. It'll just be the sounds, too. We'll at least have the courtesy to close the door. We're not complete animals.

My eyes fly open to Mar standing over me, as she pats my cheek. I'm guessing I passed out after my second drink. "Your wild ass didn't drug me again, did you?" I fake gasp like it would be the end of the world if she were to do it again. Not being able to hold my chuckle any longer, I cover my mouth when she looks taken aback.

"I wouldn't waste a drugging… we're on a plane." Her brows are furrowed, making it sound like I should know better. "Come on, we're going to test out this bedroom. I need you awake to put that mouth of yours to good use," she says loud enough for every person on the damn plane to hear, well, except the still passed-out Blair. Mar grabs my hand and starts dragging Mack and I to the back of the plane.

Mack's grinning from ear to ear, knowing exactly what kind of show she's about to put on for these poor flight attendants and Vin. We walk into the bedroom, and if it wasn't for the constant wind noise from the plane, you wouldn't even know this was a bedroom on a plane. Mar practically shoves us into the room and shuts the door behind us. "Strip. Nice and slow." She climbs up onto the bed, grabbing all the pillows and stacking them against the headboard. She crosses her arms across her chest, covering the picture of The Weeknd that's on her cropped T-shirt.

Like trained male strippers, we both grab the back of our T-shirts and pull them over our heads in one swift move. Mack doesn't know where to hold his attention. I can tell he wants to eye fuck me, but he's waiting for Mar's next command like it's his only source of oxygen. "Be good boys and put on a show for Mama." She really took to the "Mama" name, and to say it makes my cock twitch is an understatement. Something about it sends my breeding kink into space, but without the spawns that come from it…

We've all had the kid talk. Mack and I never wanted them beforehand, but it was something we were open to considering if it was a deal breaker for Mar. She never wanted any either, and now being the head of the Russians, that's the last thing she wants is to bring an innocent soul into this world for it to possibly be used as a pawn. We decided to surprise Mar with vasectomies when we get home for a late wedding gift.

Nothing says thanks for marrying me like cream pies without the worries… right?

Grabbing Mack by his arm, I pull him to me, smashing

my lips to his. I slide my other hand around his back, running it up to grip the back of his head. I pull away enough to mumble over his lips, "I've missed this, Baby Boy." He runs his hands up and down my chest, teasing the waistband of my joggers.

I look over to Mar, and she's stripped her leggings off and is still sitting up but both knees are dropped out to the sides, leaving her plump pussy on display for us. Mack's the first to come out of the trance she always seems to have us in. "Fuck, Ma'am, can we?"

She retorts right back, "Can you what?"

"Can we have a taste?" I ask instead because I can't go another minute without her on me. She nods her head, and I strip out of the rest of my clothes before lying horizontally across the end of the bed. "Baby Boy, did you wear your plug for Daddy?"

He whimpers, "Yes, Daddy." Turning around so I have a full view of his perfect plugged ass, he pulls his pants down. Mar and I groan at the sight as she climbs on top of my face.

Her favorite ride.

Taking both of my hands and placing them on either side of her pussy, spreading her wide. "This pretty cunt's already dripping for us." I use my flat tongue to drag it from her dripping hole to clit until she's rocking her hips, using me the way she needs.

Mar keeps the commands coming in between moans. "Mack, pull that plug free and sit on Percy's pretty cock. I want to see that hole of yours stretch to take him."

He climbs on top of my thighs with the bottle of lube, squirting some onto my dick while pulling the plug free with his other hand. I suck Mar's clit into my mouth, causing her hands to fly to my hair. "Yes, *Papochka,* just like that." She lifts up and looks down at me, still latched onto her, and I pull it between my teeth. She sucks in a breath as I spread her open even further, then I feel Mack notching my cock to his entrance.

I'm pushing two fingers into her, finding her G-spot with ease, while telling both of them, "My future wife is smothering me with her pussy, and my future husband is sinking onto my cock." A guttural moan leaves me as Mack fully seats himself, and I keep going, "Come for me, Mama, then get on our good boys cock. I want him filling you while I'm filling him."

I'm grinding back and forth on Percy's huge cock, all while watching Mar completely come undone on his face. She's using him exactly the way he likes. [1] Hopefully these poor flight attendants were briefed on who we were…

Marcello had to give them a warning, right?

No one can give us a bedroom on a plane and not expect us to fuck in it. Vin's bound to kick our asses when we walk out of here… non-consenting kink is his least favorite, and that's exactly what we're doing to the staff on this plane.

I can't find it in me to worry about that right now. Mar scoots back off Percy's face and backs that plump ass right up to me. Giving her a quick pat, practically begging her, I ask, "Ma'am, can I have a quick taste before you sit on my cock. I want to see if Daddy did a good enough job." I smile down at Percy right before her ass is covering my face as she straightens her legs and bends all the way over.

---

1. Mask Off - Future

The gasp that leaves me doesn't even sound real from the complete shock of her taking my cock into her mouth while upside down. That turns me feral. I suck her swollen clit into my mouth, causing her to scream out, and I start moving my hips again on Percy. I feel her spit dripping down me, coating my balls. She pops off my cock, pulling away from my mouth to tell me, "Had to get my cock nice and wet."

She's correct—my cock is hers. No questions or protests will come from me.

She's leaning over, almost flat on Percy, and I'm openly appreciating her beautiful body. Every bit of cellulite, stretch marks, and rolls makes up the obsession I have for this woman. I've always had a deep appreciation for women and what their bodies are capable of. I grab the base of my cock to line it up with her. I rush out, "Are you ready, Sovereign?" She doesn't bother to answer me. One flick of her hips and her glorious cunt has me swallowed up. I grab two hand fulls of her hips and ass to give them an appreciative shake while moaning, "Fuck I love these."

Percy pulls his mouth off of one of Mar's tits, instructing me, "Ride that cock of mine, Baby Boy, and fuck our future wife as she deserves."

And I do just that.

* * *

We wake up in a slight panic at the knock on the door, but the flight attendant's soft voice comes through the shut door, "We're about an hour out from landing. If possible, could you make your way to your seats?" We're all up, quickly moving around to find our clothes and trying not to look like absolute train wrecks. We walk out of the room to head up to our seats, when I hear the slow claps coming from Blair and Vin…

Vin is sporting a massive erection, and Blair is practically panting. Oh my god… they were just fooling around! Vin's voice is pure gravel when he says, "I would've paid good money to see what you three were doing in there…"

Mar responds immediately with the quip, "Oh, lots of people do."

He smirks at Mar's comment. "Also, I covered for you by telling the flight attendants to head to the front of the plane so they didn't have to listen to all that. Non-consenting voyeurism is never good…" I'm sure that's the reason he told them to go up there, and it has nothing to do with the blushing Blair beside him and the raging boner in his pants.

I snark over my shoulder as I sit back in my seat, "Thanks, Vin. Looks like you two were having some fun too."

* * *

I'm right behind Mar, walking down the steps, finally setting foot in Bora Bora, and it's breathtakingly beautiful. We're not technically getting married due to laws pretty much everywhere taking issue with multiple spouses… but we are having a commitment ceremony, and that's all I could ever ask for. Percy and Mar are the only people I could ever see myself with in this lifetime.

We hop on the boat for a quick ride to the overwater bungalows. The crystal-clear water below us is unreal when looking over the side of the boat. I know it's deep, but it doesn't seem like it is being able to see the bottom of the sea floor so clearly. We pull up to the docks that lead to the beach, which will eventually lead us to the bungalows we can see over in the distance.

Blair looks like she's on the verge of puking as we're docking. I check in on her, "Blair, you good?" She just nods her head at me, as if she opens her mouth, she'll spew. Vin's rubbing her back, being adorable as fuck. This side of him is the cutest shit I've ever seen, and I'm really wondering why these two aren't already together.

My vacation planner booked us the biggest villa they offer to make sure we have enough space for all the honeymoon activities we want… but you never know. We might end up putting on a show.

We have champagne glasses in our hands, and we're sent on our way down the walkway to our villas. Mar's leading the way like she always does, and I'm watching in awe at this woman with Percy beside me. As I look over at him, I see he is wearing the same look of amazement as me, with the smallest of smiles pulling at his lips. I wrap my hand around the back of his neck, murmuring, "I love you so much, Percy."

We all look up in amazement when we reach the last bungalow on the walkway. This place is huge. It looks to be at least two stories, surrounded by the clear water. Mar swings the door open, and the inside of the bungalow is just as stunning. My eyes immediately go to the floor-to-ceiling glass windows that lead to the deck, where you can easily jump into the turquoise waters. We have a huge pool and a hammock over the water as well. Everything is wood, keeping the Polynesian vibe throughout the whole villa. Blair and Vin head up the stairs to claim their room, and we head to the master suite.

It's a huge open room that flows into the bathroom, which opens up to another deck that looks out to the deeper side of the ocean. Luckily, we're facing away from the other bungalows.

Hopefully we won't have any complaints when we're fucking out here.

Mar throws her bag onto the bed and turns to me, saying, "Luchik, I have a surprise for you."

"Yes, yes, yes!" I start clapping my hands together and questioning what the gift is, "What is it, Ma'am? Hold on, let me guess!" Mar looks as bored as ever, but she waits for my guesses. "Is it a new strapless strap-on? Or maybe that suctioning pocket pussy I've been eyeing?"

She pulls it out of the bag, and I know I'm in for a hell of a week.

I give him a wicked. "Nope. A cage for that cock of yours to be punished. I will have it hard when I want, and only when I want. If you're not in my sight, the cage is on." I take a breath, then nod my head toward Percy, "He doesn't get you hard either."

"Ugh, what am I being punished for?" Mack stomps his foot down like he's pissed, but I can see the outline of his dick through his pants… he loves this shit.

"Well, *Luchik*… where do I begin?" I let that float through the air for a second, then start counting on my fingers all the shit he's been doing, testing every boundary he could. "You called Marcello and planned this trip from an off-the-wall comment from me, promised the subs a live while here, and if I see one more aesthetic picture of a wedding, I think I'll pull an '07 Brittany." I can't deny and say his excitement for our elopement doesn't fill my stomach with butterflies, but I know he loves these "punishments" too… so he continues to act like a brat anytime he can.

"Fine," he huffs, crossing his arms over his broad chest. I raise my brows at him, and he adds, "*Ma'am.*"

"I'm going to need that cock soft, so I can put your cage on and lock it up. I have a massage scheduled with Blair in about thirty minutes," I taunt him while moving to unpack my bag and throw my swimsuit on.

I pull my shirt over my head, and my shorts hit the floor. "Mar… Mama," Percy groans. "Baby Boy's cock is never going to go down with your gorgeous body on display." He's shamelessly running his hand over his cock through his pants.

We have seen a pick-up in activity on the guys' accounts because it's Halloween time, and with that comes the masked men craze. I always say it's a year-round thing, but the attention they get during October is astonishing. You'd never know it would be such a big thing, but a mask kink is more common than you think…

"Well, guess what, *Papochka?* That's not my issue," I mock Percy while I pull on my swimsuit bottoms, which happen to be a literal thong… only covering the necessary bits. My top is nothing more than a string bikini, and I shuffle over in front of Mack. "Be a good boy and tie Mama up."

"Oh, if only you'd let us tie you up," Percy murmurs under his breath, and my right eye twitches at him. He's speeding up, rubbing that big cock of his.

"In your wildest dreams, Percy. Now get that cock out; I want to see you come on your boyfriend's face before I leave." I spin around once Mack's tied the back of my swimsuit up and whisper in his ear, "And you better keep that cock soft." I run my hand up and down him. "This isn't feeling too soft to me, *Luchik*…"

Mack throws his head back, groaning, "Please, Ma'am,

don't tease me. It's going to be bad enough sucking Daddy's cock."

Percy steps up behind me, moving my hair to the side as he kisses up my back to my neck. "You sit over in that chair and tell our good boy what you want to see."

Gripping Mack in my hand through his shorts and biting down on his huge trap muscle, he lets out an animalistic moan. "Percy, get your cock in his mouth. He's enjoying this a little too much for my liking." I feel his cock jump in my hand, and I rear back, smacking it. The hiss leaves his lips, followed by a crooked smile. "I've got ten minutes; you better have Percy's cum covering your face within that time."

By the time I sit down in the large wicker chair in the corner, Percy's pants are around his ankles. I let out a low whistle in appreciation of these two. Still, to this day, I don't understand how I pulled the two of them, but here they are at my feet, worshiping me as they should.

Percy practically growls, "Open up for Daddy. Nice and wide. Tongue out." He starts to slap his leaking cock onto Mack's tongue.

Mack lets out a groan while looking up at Percy. "Please… Daddy. I need it. I need y—" Percy cuts him off before he can finish his sentence, grabbing the sides of his head, and starts pounding into his mouth with brutal thrusts. The gagging has me laying back in the chair, pulling my feet up below my ass, and sliding my bikini bottoms over, freeing my pussy. I see Mack's eyes on me, and I bite my bottom lip while running my fingers over my throbbing pussy lips.

Bringing my fingers to my mouth, I'm putting on a show for him, but I catch Percy's attention from the sloppy sucking noises leaving me. Percy immediately barks out, "Absolutely not. Turn and face the other way. I get to watch our wife finger fuck herself. You're getting punished, Baby Boy." Mack lets a whimper leave him while he turns the other way, and I'm enjoying the butterflies swarming in my stomach from hearing "my wife."

Dipping my fingers through my slit, I ensure I'm nice and wet. "Fuck our good boy's throat, *Papochka,* and I want your cum on his face, so I can lick him clean," I instruct him and start to feverishly circle my clit.

[1] Percy has both hands encasing Mack's head and is thrusting in and out. He's staying so deep in his throat that I know Mack will be sore after this. The tears lining Mack's eyes spring up as Percy says, "Cry for me, Baby Boy. You're so pretty when you cry for Daddy." That sends me spiraling over the edge… coming faster than I ever have.

As I'm coming down from my orgasm, Percy's grunting while Mack reaches up, rolling and pulling Percy's balls in between his fingers. That does him in. He screams, "Fuck, Mack, yes!" Pulling out of his mouth and shooting his load all over his pretty face.

I stand up and pull my swimsuit back into place, sauntering to Mack to fulfill my end of the deal. He's still on his knees, and I tilt his face up to mine, while I grit out, "You pathetic slut. Look at you…" Bending at my waist, I lick from his jawline to his cheekbone, cleaning him up. "Coming in your shorts while your boyfriend made you cry with his big cock down your throat." I lick up the other side, over his lips, then place a kiss on them. I give him a smack on the cheek, grab the cock cage from on the bed, and nod at him to pull his shorts down. I lock his quickly softening cock up, then whisper to him, "Be a good boy while I'm gone, and you'll get your next surprise when I get back."

---

1.   PRETTY WHEN U CRY - PLVTINUM

* * *

"Spill your guts, Blair. I need the nasty details, and I need them now." We're out on the beach, lying side by side on the massage tables. I didn't miss the noises that were coming from upstairs in the bungalow earlier while the guys and I were fucking around.

Blair sighs. "You know what we were doing, Mar. Don't make me explain it all. I'm sure these two massage therapists do not want to hear every detail."

My massage therapist says, "Ms. Sovereign, we are under an NDA. Anything said stays between us."

"See, Blair. And our guard dog is out of earshot. Spill!" Vin came to the beach with us for protection, and I can't deny it is nice being able to relax and have some much-needed girl time. And what's better than getting to the nitty-gritty about what Blair and Vin have been up to? This was my plan all along anyway… getting these two together.

"It's nothing new between us… You've known about the crush I had on him for ages, but one night, he came to the apartment to make sure I was okay after something happened with Ellie, and the rest was history." She takes a breath, and she knows that's not going to be enough information for my nosy ass. Then she starts to spill the shit I've been wondering, "I built up the courage to take the kink quiz on Sins website, then decided to get a membership to explore what my body was really craving." She's staring out into the water, lost in the memory, smiling, and I can't get over how much she's changed and grown over the past couple of years we've known each other.

"Shit, Blair, had you fucked someone before Vin?!"

"Marfa Sovereign! What do you take me for? Of course, I had. Was it ever good? Fuck no."

I release my breath. "I was so scared… I had been telling you all my wild stories since I've known you. I'm surprised you didn't go running."

"I always wanted to be as confident as you, and you've for sure rubbed off on me, but I needed to find the person that brought it out of me… That just so happens to be my uncle's best friend." She turns back, looking at me. "He plays my body like a goddamn instrument, Mar. And it's not even the sex, it's everything before it. Plus, watching people in the club has opened my eyes to my sexuality as well. There's just so much up in the air."

"Well, use this trip away to figure everything out. You know you could've come to me to talk about all this, right? I don't judge, you know that. And I would never tell Marcello… Unless you wanted me to." I let out a chuckle at the fear in her eyes. "Okay, maybe we won't jump the gun on that yet."

Blair snorts. "Thank fuck everyone is deathly afraid of Marcello, or we would've been ratted out by now. We've been parading around Sins' like it's our jobs." Yeah… I would not want to be the one spoiling the news to him that his niece is getting railed by his best friend, until her soul begs to leave her body.

Whoever breaks that news to him better be ready to say bye to their organs…

Mack and I are walking up the walkways toward the beach to meet with the ceremony planner to make sure they have everything settled for tomorrow. We're passing the resort's main pool where everyone is allowed to swim and, lo-and-behold, there's our pilot leaning against the poolside watching as the two flight attendants suck face in front of him.

"Oh shit, Percy, look, it's th—" I shush him while we keep watching the three of them, being absolute creeps.

[1]Picking them up in one arm each, he spins with the two women to push them against the poolside without even breaking them apart.

Fuck they're hot together. And knowing they're co-workers with their boss…

Out of the corner of my eye, I see Mack bring his finger to his mouth to let out a wolf whistle. That grabs their attention, and he yells out, "Get it! You three look so h—"

---

1. Right Here - Chase Atlantic

I throw my hand up in apology. "Carry on, sorry about him." I'm shoving him toward the building where I'm sure the planner is waiting on us, and start to tear into him, "Your ass never learns, do you? A cage around your cock, and you're still looking for more punishment?"

He shrugs. "They needed some encouragement."

"I think they had all they needed." Thankfully it looked like they had been drinking. Empty margarita glasses were beside them on the pool deck. Let's just hope they don't remember that little interaction in the morning.

"Loe?" We open the door to the resort center, and Mack walks up to one of the people who looks like they work here.

"Mack and Percy?" She reaches her hand out to shake.

I grab her hand and give it a shake. "It's so nice to meet you, Loe, and thank you so much for showing us the ceremony space beforehand. This one right here has been stressing over every little detail."

Mack points to his chest where a name tag would be, conveying to me, "Percy, just so you know, they use non-binary pronouns." Mack smiles at them, and they return a beaming one. I give them both a nod, and we all carry on to the outside space.

Fuck I feel bad gendering them in my head.

We follow Loe through the huge sliding glass doors that face the beautiful beach. Not even fifty steps out the doors, our feet hit the sand as we toe off our shoes. The setup itself isn't anything special, just a blocked-off section of the beach with a basic arch and a couple of chairs set out, letting the scenery be the focal point. The lagoon is breath-taking enough on its own. We have a boat tour booked for the day after the wedding to snorkel the reef that also lines the island. Before an abundant amount of research last week, I had no clue Bora Bora has a damn lagoon…

I learn something new every day.

Loe is explaining tomorrow's schedule and the time we will all need to arrive, and all I can focus on is how lucky I am that my soul was brought here to live this life. Mack is fully immersed in the conversation, and I find myself staring at the side of his head, openly appreciating the faded sides of his haircut and the bleached-out longer hair on the top that Blair has perfected.

The thought hits me, like it has so many times over the past week.

I get to marry my two best friends—both of them.

My love for each of them is so different, and I never think there's a way to fall in love with them any deeper, then I watch them with each other. My heart nearly bursts every time I see them showing one another love. No matter what the law sees our relationship or commitment as, it doesn't matter. They'll both always and forever be mine.

We wrap things up with Loe and stop by the restaurant on the resort to ensure it's also good to go after the ceremony. Mack had the whole place rented out... for the five people who will be attending our wedding. But I didn't rain on his parade. This is the only time we're doing this, so we might as well go big... *right?*

We walk hand-in-hand along the boardwalk back to our bungalow. [2]I sigh, "We needed this vacation so badly, Baby Boy."

"That I can agree with." He looks up at me with the sun setting behind his head over the horizon and the glow omitting from his green eyes, making him look ethereal.

---

2. Life is Good (feat. Drake) - Future, Drake

"But I can't wait to get out of this cock cage." And there go the serious thoughts scrambling from my head.

"That's if I don't tell Mar about the stunt you pulled at the pool…" I tease, but switch back to my serious tone. "I know I don't say this enough, but I am so deeply thankful for you and Mar. Having both of you doesn't seem possible, but it is. I have to pinch myself daily when thinking about it. I love you Mack, beyond words… beyond lifetimes, and beyond anything our soul can comprehend." I stop in my tracks, pushing him against the railing on the boardwalk.

I grab his face, running my thumbs over his smile lines. Those little lines truly show how happy he always is. I place my lips against his, barely holding back the need to ravage him in the most animalistic way. He pulls away enough to murmur, "I love you so much, Percy. I never thought I would get married or find my person, but I've been lucky enough to find two. You both have woven into my soul, and I hope the thread never gets pulled out."

"Come on, Baby, let's go get our missing piece." I'm sure she and Blair have gotten into all kinds of trouble since we've been gone.

We walk into a quiet bungalow, and I look over at Percy, who is smirking. "Let's get everything set up and surprise Mar." Walking around the lower level of the bungalow, Percy and I are setting up our recording equipment. Mar hates the setup portion, so she'll be excited that we have it done already.

I was smart enough to tease the followers with a "honeymoon but make it Halloween" on the live last week. Since we're masked cosplayers, October is always a big month for our streaming. But honestly, we have such a loyal fan base behind us year-round.

The spooky holiday just brings in the new, unaware mask-kink folk.

We peeked out the big windows on the way into the master bedroom and saw Vin on the deck with the girls, watching while they jump into the beautiful water right outside our room. They're all laughing, looking like they are having the time of their lives.

* * *

Percy is pulling his black cargo pants over his thighs, and I groan, "The genes your mother blessed you with…" I do the chef's kiss hand motion and add the lip-smacking noise of a kiss. "I've truly never seen a better physique on a man. And I'm lucky enough to call you mine. I get to worship those thighs any time I want."

[1]*I wonder how questionable I would sound asking him to smash my head between them?*

"I may have gotten the thighs, Baby Boy, but your upper body is beyond anything mine will ever be. Your arms. Your shoulders… and don't get me started on your fucking back." He bites his fist, being more playful than usual. As he processes my statement again, he asks, "How do you know it was my mom and not my dad's genes?!"

I chuckle. "Because your mom has those same thighs…" He gasps at my answer, right as Blair, Mar, and Vin walk through the sliding glass door to our room.

We have our cargo pants on with the holsters strapped onto our thighs, and our masks are lying on the bed when Blair questions, "Oh. My. God… Are you all about to film?!" She almost sounds scared, but I don't miss the glint of curiosity in her eyes. It's so wild seeing Vin so caught up in a woman. I don't know what I expected out of him, but it for sure wasn't being brought to his knees by anyone. And on the flip side, I couldn't imagine anyone better for Blair. I've known her for what feels like a lifetime. She's been my hairdresser for the longest time, and watching her come out of her shell with Vin has been nothing but amazing.

I'm very curious how everyone will handle this situation, though. The devil knows we're nothing but exhibitionists. Mar's the first one to answer Blair, "You two are

---

1. Freek-A-Leek - Petey Pablo

free to do whatever you want. Stay and watch, go into the living room and just listen, or vacate the property…. we'll be loud, I can guarantee that much, but yes, we're about to film."

Blair turns to face Vin, practically begging, "Can we stay and watch?! I want to see Mar work. And you know I love to watch." The feral fucking grin that Vin is sporting has to be the same one the people he "takes care of" see before their last breath is taken…

"Of course we can stay, *Terremoto.*" He looks over at me first, asking, "Are you okay with us staying?"

"Fuck yes!" I immediately answer him.

"I am, too. Just be warned, we are into some wild shit, and the subscribers are even wilder. If it gets to be too much, we will not judge you if you need to step out." Blair nods at Percy's words as Vin walks them over to the over-sized wicker seat in the corner.

We have the stream up on the TV so we can see it from the bed. Our normal two cameras are also up on their tripods: one at the foot of the bed and one on the side closest to the wall.

"You still have my cock caged, *Luchik?*"

"Yes, Ma'am. Do I get to get out of it now?!"

She barks back immediately, "No." I look over at Blair, and her brows are nearly touching her hairline.

Mar walks over to her bag, pulls her glowing red horns out, and places them in front of each bun she has her hair in. Percy and I slide our masks into place. He clicks the button to begin the stream, announcing, "We're live."

Mar is still in her swimsuit, and now that I'm looking, Blair and Vin are as well. She's sitting on his lap but paying rapt attention to what's happening with us.

Mar gives Percy instructions, "König, tie up your slutty

little boyfriend. I don't care how, as long as he's lying on his back. I need access to that pretty face of his."

Oh fuck yes, this is going to be fun.

I'm about to jump onto the bed, but Percy practically growls, "Clothes off now, Ghost." I'm stripping my holster off my leg, unbuttoning my pants, pulling my pants and briefs down.

The hiss leaves my lips, and that spurs Mar on. "The poor slut is sensitive. Read some chats for us, Ghost."

I do as I'm told, not needing any more punishment, so I start to read:

> $300 - @SPREAD_MY_CHEEKS
>
> Happy Honeymoon & Halloween to my favorite trio. I can't wait for the wedding fucking!

> $69 - @WALK.ME.LIKE.A.DOG
>
> OMG! Is that a cock cage, Ghost?!

Mar starts answering back to the subscriber, "That is indeed a cock cage. Ghost can't be hard without me."

I continue to read:

> $18 - @USEMYHOLES
>
> Not fair! I want a cock cage, Mommy!!!

I'm lying on the bed, just as Mar and Percy instructed, and she explains, "And that includes when he's around his soon-to-be husband, alone. My two whores will do anything for an orgasm… And all those orgasms are mine on this trip." She turns around to face the bed when she has finally dug out whatever she needs from her duffle bag filled with sex toys.

It's my favorite bag on the face of the planet.

My eyes practically bug out of my head when I see

what she's holding. "Why the hell do you have a hockey helmet?!"

Percy snorts when he hears what I asked. I'm sure he's been plotting and scheming this whole ordeal, but I can't lie and say I'm not interested in why she's holding said helmet. "This right here is your new headgear for the live that you signed us up to do... while away doing our commitment ceremony and our goddamn honeymoon."

The sinister smile covering her face has my toes curling. Knowing what's about to happen is going to be pure bliss. It was very bratty of me to offer the live to the subs last week, but it was too good an opportunity.

Especially with it being October. She knows I couldn't resist.

This helmet has a cage on the bottom that will cover my mouth and nose, but the top part is transparent and will be over my eyes, allowing me to see.

Fuck I might make this a part of my normal gear...

This is going to look cool as shit with my Ghost mask below it. She comes to straddle me, lifting the back of my head to put on the helmet and buckle it into place.

[2]"I'll keep the gag out of your mouth for now, but you keep the brat shit up, and I'll stuff your mouth full." She thinks that over for a second, then starts thinking out loud, "I would like to see you drooling on yourself, now that I think about it." She narrows her eyes at me but decides to let me be... *for now.*

Percy's climbing up onto the bed, rope in his hand, and I'm wondering which kind he brought on the trip. The rougher the material, the better when I'm tied up. Knowing Percy, he probably brought some of each.

He loves his options.

Percy barks out his command, "Both hands on your

---

2. Big Mama - Latto

stomach." I watch as he methodically wraps the rope around my wrist, then starts wrapping it up my arms. I don't even pretend to know what the hell he's doing. One pull and this knot will come untied, and I bet he has a plan for later. I love being tied up, and thankfully, he loves doing the tying.

I zone out until I hear Blair ask Vin, "Can you teach me how to do that? Or maybe you can do it to me? I don't know what I would like more."

Vin's voice is low and pure sex. "We can teach you at Sin's. Actually, it looks like we need to bring König in to run a workshop."

Percy's head whips around, and if we could see his face under his mask, he'd be grinning from ear to ear. He answers in a surprisingly chill tone, "I would love to."

"We have some guests today, Devils." Mar has made pretty much every subscriber a Devil. Since day one, people have been so accepting of her. I'm thankful that we can come together in that way.

Percy gets done tying my arms together, then pulls them above my head, attaching them to a point on the bed frame. Mar is still on top of me, but she's dragging her swimsuit-covered pussy over my cock.

Said cock is still caged.

"Ma'am, please… I'll be a good slut for you." I pause, looking down at where our bodies are meeting. The pain of all the blood trying to make its way to my cock is unbearable, so I beg, "Mommy, pleassee, un-cage my cock. I'll be the dirtiest of sluts just for you."

"Are you a good boy for Daddy?" Percy questions Mack, and I almost laugh at Blair's jaw hanging open. Between begging me to free his cock, and now Percy's going in on him too, she doesn't know what to think. This will either make our friendship a hell of a lot stronger or send her running for the hills.

Only time will tell.

"Yessss! I'm a good boy for Daddy. I'm a good, obedient, tied-up slut." Right as he finishes the sentence, I sit up on my knees and smack the head of his dick that's sticking out of the cock cage.

He cries out, shocked, and I tease him, "Well, guess what, *Ghost*? You haven't been a good boy for Mommy. Have you?" I'm going to toy with him a little more, but I need his dick out to be able to use it.

[1]I climb off of him, slide off the bed, and head for the drawer that I know the key is in. I blurt out over my

---

1. BEG! - Vana

shoulder to Mack, "Look at our guest over there, and tell him whose slut you are."

"I'm Sovereigns fucktoy to use whenever and however she sees fit."

"That's right, *Luchik*. My free-use whore. König, plug his hole and get him stretched out for me. Also, get those damn pants off! We all want to see those meaty thighs of yours." I toss the plug and bottle of lube over to him, and he's stripping faster than I've ever seen him.

Percy climbs onto the bed, kneeling, instructing Mack on what he wants him to do, "Pull these legs up to your chest. I need to see that greedy hole of yours." He places two pillows under his ass, giving the people on the live the best view.

Blair and Vin have the best view in the house.

I start to read the chats off while Percy gets him ready:

$100 - @ALTANDMASKING

The amount of money I would pay to be those guests.

I respond to the commenter, "Yeah, they're two lucky souls, aren't they?"

$45 - @DADDYSBADBOY

Does Ghost get pegged tonight Sovereign?

I tap my chin like I'm really needing to think about it, then respond to the comment, "We'll have to see what we have in store for today…" I release the strings holding my bathing suit top, and the sound of the wet plop hitting the floor draws everyone's eyes to me. I give them a quick shake of my head, silently asking what they're staring at, like they don't constantly see this body of mine. [2]"I would

---

2. IF THERE IS A GOD, IT'S ME - PLVTINUM

ask if you like what you see, but the incoherent moaning from you two is slightly embarrassing."

They truly appreciate my body the way it should be… Honestly, most people do, but I'm sure some can't get over the fatphobia that's been ingrained in their psyche since the earliest of ages. Some people are stupid enough to vocalize those horrendous thoughts… but guess what? As long as you can love yourself, you can magnetize people into your life who love you, your body, and your soul the same way you do.

And that's exactly what I have in my life—two men who truly appreciate me for me. The power and authority I hold would be a hit to most men's egos… not theirs though. They never try to undermine me in any way, and that's all I ever could've dreamed of from a partner.

The only acceptable place for them is at my feet, willingly listening to my every command.

Percy has the plug lubbed up, and the tip of the toy pressed against Mack's waiting hole. "Baby Boy, you look so goddamn good tied up for Daddy. I can't wait to see what Sovereign has in store for us tonight." Percy starts working the toy into Mack slowly. The groans coming out of Percy have me thinking he's getting the pleasure out of this, but I know it's from making Mack feel good. The plug is finally seated in his ass, but I need to continue Mack's punishment.. He's enjoying all of this a little too much.

My hands fly to the two strings on my bottoms, and they hit the floor in the same wet plopping sound. This time, I don't care whose attention I've grabbed. I'm going to tease my sweet, bratty, *Luchik.*

Mack commands, "Come put that pretty pussy on my new helmet, Ma'am."

I pick up my swimsuit bottoms off the ground, having the perfect plan for them. I announce, "Since that was a command instead of the begging that you know I want, you can lie here with my salt water-soaked bottoms in this worthless mouth of yours." I work them under his new helmet, lifting the spandex material that covers his mouth. I push them into his mouth, and what does he do… groans. The fucker groans.

This isn't even punishment for his masochistic ass.

Percy joins in on the degrading. "Look at the drool and water already dripping down your chin and cheeks. *Pathetic.*"

Finally, I reach over the bed to unlock Mack's cock cage. It looks like it might've been painful, but it doesn't seem like it's bothering him at the moment. I run my hand up and down it, and he lets out a whimper. "Is this okay, *Luchik?*" I look him in the eyes to make sure he's telling me the truth.

He nods, due to his mouth being occupied with my swimsuit, but looks very sincere in his answer.

Percy ensures Mack is able to communicate since he can't speak or use his arms. He tells him, "Tap twice if you need to stop."

I pull the attention back to the action, telling Mack, "Actually, I need to use this mouth real quick. Make me come, Ghost." I unstrap his helmet from around his chin, lift the helmet above his mask, and pull my swimsuit out of his mouth. I don't even give him a breath before I lower onto his glorious mouth.

He doesn't waste a second, licking his flat tongue from my hole right up to my clit. His hands are still tied up above his head. I grab onto the headboard to avoid face planting, causing my whole ass to undoubtedly be on full display.

I hear Percy breathlessly speaking behind me, but I don't even bother to look at him. "Mama, you can't put that ass in my face and expect me not to overindulge." I feel his hands running down my back before landing on the globes of my ass cheeks, pulling them apart. Then his flat tongue meets Mack's on that thin piece of skin between my holes.

"Oh fuck," are the only words that can leave my mouth in between the moaning. I let go, surrendering to the pleasure pouring into my body from these two men I'm fortunate enough to soon call my husbands.

Mack has moved his focus entirely on my clit, sucking like his life depends on it. Percy is tongue-fucking my ass and is now shoving two fingers into my dripping cunt. They're playing me like the masters of pleasure that they are.

Percy's fingers are pounding into the spot I struggle to reach myself, over and over again. Add his tongue and Mack's suction, and I'm being shoved into what I can only describe as a black hole of ecstasy… and I don't ever want to see the light again.

When I finally catch my breath and return down to the planet, I look down and see the mess I've made of a certain wide-eyed, golden retriever man. "Oh, *Luchik*… look at this pretty face covered in my cum."

I watch as Mar leans down, licking Mack's face, but she doesn't stop there. She drags her tongue up the skull part of his face mask, too.

Fuck that was hot.

[1]She pulls back from Mack, pats his cheek, and murmurs to him, "Don't think you're getting out of that helmet just because you made me squirt all over that pretty face of yours."

I give her a slap on the ass, watching as it ripples from her hip to her back, then ask her, "Do you want to be fucked, Mama?"

She shakes it back and forth, and I watch practically in a trance. I give it a few extra shakes up and down with my hands and then glance at her as she finally turns around to answer me, "Duh. Let's fuck over top of Ghost's face."

She's biting her lip, obviously loving Mack being tied up and tortured without being able to touch either one of us. "As you wish," I murmur as I scoot further up Mack's

---

1. THE RIDE - Omido, Kae

body, but not before smacking the plug that's nestled between his ass cheeks.

He gasps, moaning to me, "Dadddyyy. Please."

Mar remarks, "You're begging the wrong one, Ghost." She pauses, but not long enough for him to beg her. "Seeing your boyfriend's cock going in and out of this cunt will have you begging soon enough…"

I've forgotten that Vin and Blair are over in what we've referred to as the "cuck chair" multiple times during the live. I also forgot that we're live-streaming… Mar has been too hot to take my eyes off of, and add in Mack being tied up, his glorious body on full display, I have more important things to focus on. She places his helmet back in place, strapping him up like he's about to head out on the ice for a game.

My cock is swaying heavily between my legs, and I lower myself just enough to drag it over Mack's swollen and sensitive cock. He lets out a moan at the slight touch, and I hear Vin groan behind me; I smile under my mask and turn my head to ask him, "You like that, don't you?"

Blair is spread out on his lap, leaning back on Vin, and he has his hand down the front of her swimsuit. Her head pops up off his shoulder, and she practically yells, "Fuck! What did I miss?!"

He presses his lips to her ear. "König's about to fuck your best friend over their other fiancé's face, *Terremoto*, and Ghost isn't allowed to touch."

Blair answers the question I asked earlier, "I don't know about him, but I'm loving what I'm seeing… actually, I take that back. He's loving it too by the size of the erection that's pressing between my ass cheeks."

[2]Vin growls into her neck. "Keep it up, and I'll make you beg for this cock like I did the last time."

Blair wastes no time snarking back, "Or I can just call Noah, and he can talk me through an orgasm, and I'll make you watch."

That gets Mar's attention. She whips her head around so fast I'm sure she's got minor whiplash. "Who?! What?! When?! Why do I not know about this? Noah as in Noah Noah?!"

"Later! Preferably not in front of the audience!" She waves her hand out to the cameras and the TV, narrowing her eyes at Mar.

"Fine! Now, König, fuck me!" I'm sure the chat's going wild right now from that little snippet from Blair and Vin.

I take my dick in my hand, running it up and down Mar's soaking slit. A hiss escapes me as my tip barely breaches her opening. "Fuck, Mama, this tight cunt is begging me to wreck it."

"Yeah, it is. Now wreck it, *Papochka*," she retorts immediately.

With a punishing grip, I start to pound into her. We're above Mack's face—well, his helmet more so—and I can feel my balls on the cage. I question Mack, "How do you like the view down there, Baby Boy?"

"It's the best thing I've ever laid my eyes on. I get to watch my wife's—as of tomorrow—perfect pussy, swallow up my soon-to-be husband's cock."

I groan at Mack's words, knowing he's loving every second of all of this, but the thought of him watching us from his vantage point without being able to do anything has my release much closer than I'm ready for. I reach around to find Mar's clit, so I can pull her over the edge

---

2. Backseat - Daniel Di Angelo

with me. "Our slut can't help out with your pleasure today… he's a little tied up at the moment, and I need you coming before I do, Mama."

She's still holding onto the headboard fucking back onto me. My fingers are moving back and forth at a wicked pace over her swollen bundle of nerves. The motion of my hand is moving Mack's helmet and head back and forth, and I think that sight is what ends up pushing Mar to come undone. "Fuck, fuck, fucckkk, *Papochka*! I'm coming!"

With a clenched jaw, pulling out to the tip, I grit out, "Where do you want it, Sovereign?" Fuck I can't hold it any longer; I don't give her a choice. "I'm filling this begging, breedable cunt, Mama."

As she comes down from her orgasm, she looks back at me with raised brows, questioning, "Did I say to come in me?" I give her a shake of my head, and I watch as an unhinged smile forms on her face. "Sit on the bed. You only get to watch now, and keep that mouth shut, or I *will* get my ball gag out."

I watch as she hovers over Mack's face. She starts talking to him, "Open your mouth, Ghost, and watch as our boyfriend's cum drips into your mouth." I hear Blair let a shameless moan out while I move over beside a still-tied-up Mack. Honestly, I'm getting an even better view of what's happening. Mar shouts at me, "Read some chats, König."

$27 - @MUFF_DIV3R

Sovereign we've been good, König hasn't been though… Can you tie him up? Pretty please.

I drag out the begging tone when reading the last couple of words. A part of me wants to be tied up while watching whatever she has in store for Mack tonight.

Mar's finally unstrapping my helmet, pulling the rope's tail, and letting my arms free. "König… I know I didn't tell you to stop reading the chats." She gets to her bag of goodies and pulls out the ball gag. My brows shoot up, but she starts talking to Percy again. "You know what? Since you won't use that pretty mouth for anything useful, it might as well be wide open."

She pulls her strapless strap-on out of the bag and struts back over to the bed. Her heavy tits sway, and the protruding fluff above her hips jiggles with each step. Saliva pools in my mouth from admiring the work of art her body truly is.

She's all women.

My fists are balled up, trying to keep from reaching out and grabbing those hips to run my hands all over her exquisite body. I'm trying to listen and behave, being her good boy, but fuck is it hard when that supple skin of hers is calling out to me.

Fuck I love her so much.

[1] *My powerful queen.*

My eyes never leave her as she climbs on the bed and moves over me, prowling toward Percy. He's sitting with his back against the headboard, legs out in front of him, and she moves to straddle him.

I can already see his cock getting hard again, but I doubt she'll let him come again anytime soon. She teases him, running her cum-dripping cunt up and down his cock. With his mask still hanging over his face, she bites her way over his jaw until she reaches his ear, whispering, "My little whore's speechless now, isn't he?" Percy throws his head back, trying to fight, but giving in to her.

I eat this shit up, watching them battle it out for power.

She gives his ear lobe one more tug with her teeth before pulling the ball gag in front of his mouth. Finally, she lifts the bottom of Percy's mask so we can see everything below his nose. I admire his perfect bearded jawline and that pulsing neck vein beside his flawless Adam's apple. I let out a shameless groan that pulls their eyes to me, but doesn't distract her from her plans. Once the gag is strapped behind his head, she hovers right over it. She licks the outside of the gag, then his lips, and tells him, "Drool nice and pretty for me König… or should I say, *Daddy*?" Percy lets out a feral moan causing my dick to react.

Mar scoots back on her knees, looks down at Percy's now rock-hard cock, and gives it one languid lick. I beg, unable to take it any longer, "Ma'am, can I please move?"

She sits on her knees and starts crawling toward me on the bed. I don't say a word, just watch in amazement as those tits sway back and forth. If I said anything, I'd be crawling around this island for the rest of our trip. "I have plans for you, *Luchik.*"

---

1. SACRILEGIOUS - PLVTINUM

CHAPTER TWENTY-FOUR

I hope those plans include that strapless strap-on…

"Now keep being a good boy and read some chats while I get my cock ready for you to ride," she says, as she's lays down with her head at the end of the bed. She's spread out between Percy and I, and we've got the best view as she starts to work the G-spot stimulating end into herself. I haven't seen this toy yet; it might be new, or it could just be that this woman has so many sex toys she pulls them out of that bag like a goddamn magician pulls rabbits out of their hat.

I start to read the chats out loud:

> $16 - @I.LIKE.BIG.DICKS.&.I.CAN.NOT.LIE
>
> We're about to get the best view with Ghost riding Mommy.

> $48 - @LICKME_SUCKME_FUCKME
>
> König looks so good with that big cock leaking all over his stomach. I would pay so much money for that man's cum to be shipped to me.

Mar answers back immediately to the commenter, "You all know better than that. All of König's cum belongs to this little cum slut reading your worthless chats."

She's lubing up her silicone cock and has the remote to control the clit suction for herself, and I'm sure my end vibrates too… this is my favorite. Mar getting her pleasure from fucking me. "Climb up on Mommy's cock, Ghost." Percy lets out something between a whimper and a moan. I peek over at him, and his drool is dripping down his chin and neck. Mar laughs, but there's no humor behind it. "Oh, König… you look pathetic. But at least you get to watch our pretty husband ride my cock."

"Fuck… why is this so hot?" Blair grits out like she's in

pain and winded; looking at them, I'm shocked for a second. Vin's cock-deep inside her.

Goddamn, they look good together, though.

Chuckling, I say to them, "I'm surprised it took you two this long to start fucking."

[2]Mar can't help herself and turns her head. "Damn, bitch, ride that cock! I've never been prouder." She wipes her fake tears, then tells me, "You've got some competition, *Luchik…* Come show Mama what you got."

I crawl up her body, lifting the bottom of my mask to lay a gentle kiss on her lips, really appreciating how soft and plump they are. I kiss her neck, trailing down to her chest, stopping to suck in one of her mahogany buds. My other hand grabs as much of her other tit as I can fit in my calloused palm, pinching and rolling her other nipple. I bite down, and I hear her suck in a breath. I let it come with me while I back away, eventually letting go with a pop to smile at her. "Okay, I'm ready now. I needed to get them in my mouth. They've been teasing me all day."

I get to my knees and slowly pull the plug out that has been keeping me stretched and ready, tossing it to the floor.

We have to remember to find that, or the housekeepers will have a hell of a story to tell if not.

Looking down at her perfect pussy and running my hand over the silicone cock, I tell her, "I love riding your cock like this, Mommy."

"I should've gagged you too…" she sighs, but her eyes never leave my body.

Swinging my leg over her stomach and leaning forward, I start to slide my hole over the cock. Percy is groaning so much, so I turn my head to tease, "You wish this ass was about to swallow that big cock of yours, don't

---

2. Traphouse - Tory Lanez, Nyce

you, Daddy?" All I hear is the smack before it registers that Mar just smacked the head of my cock again. I gasp in shock, but it quickly turns into a moan.

Fuck, why do I like that so much?!

"Quit teasing him. That's my job, and if you keep it up, you won't be coming for the rest of the trip," she warns.

Mar is holding onto the base of the cock, making sure it's steady for me. I line my hole up and slowly let it breach me. My head is thrown back in bliss as I take it to the hilt. I have my hands braced on her calves as I stand on my feet, bouncing up and down, getting my pleasure anyway she'll let me have it.

"Look at that big cock flopping up and down for me, and that slutty hole of yours is sucking me right in," she says as she reaches for the remote to turn the toy on. "You're taking my cock so well, Ghost." She reaches up and starts rolling my balls in her fingers, and fuck if that doesn't have the orgasm at the back of my thighs, but I want to hold it off as long as I can.

Trying to distract her, I blurt out, "And look at those big tits shaking for me, Sovereign. Is my hole being greedy enough for you?"

She groans, loving me asking if I'm doing things to her liking. "Such a good boy for me, Ghost. Giving the subscribers exactly what they want for their favorite holiday. One masked man riding a fake cock, and another drooling around a ball gag. As all men should be... quiet, hot as fuck, and breedable." She moans like she doesn't have us like that twenty-four-seven.

I can see Blair slamming down on Vin's cock; getting to watch them in person and the noises in this room are enough to send anyone into a spiraling into a mess of orgasms.

"Use my cock to milk that greedy prostate of yours. I want you milked dry. Ride Mommy's cock, yes, just like that." She flips the vibration on, and I immediately gasp. Percy is incoherently begging and slobbering beside us, but I don't even turn to look. I can see him clear as day on the TV being streamed to millions of people.

My eyes are darting around the room, not knowing where to look. There's us on the TV, Mar's swollen pussy gripping her end of the toy, her tits bouncing every time I slam down on her, or Blair and Vin in the goddamn cuck chair.

Or should I say fuck chair?

Mar grips my cock in a strangling hold, and I beg, "Please, please make me come for you, Ma'am." She smacks my ass as I ride up and down on her, and that spurs me on.

I'm riding Mar's cock like my life depends on it, and it might just depend on it. I need to come about as bad as I need my next breath. I'm making eye contact with Vin while Blair's head is tipped back on his shoulder as she falls apart for him for at least the third time since I've been paying attention to them. He's wearing a wicked smile, and it seems like this might be his favorite thing to do… pulling pleasure out of the ones he's with.

While others are watching… the kinky bastard does own a sex club, after all.

Mar turns the vibration up on both of our ends, and from the sounds of it, she's also turned up the suction on her clit. I hear Vin practically growling into Blair's neck, "I'm going to fill this tight little cunt of mine so full of my cum. Breed you until you can't fucking walk, and then take pictures of this glistening cunt so your hacker slut can find them." He bites down on her shoulder, and they're both screaming out while coming, and that's enough to send me right over the edge.

My cum is spraying Mar's stomach and hand, and that sends her over the edge, finally seeing me get my pleasure. She flips the power off on the toy as I slide off it. Mar removes the gag from Percy, and I strut over to tell the subscribers thanks for watching, and we'll be back on when we get home.

I thought it would be awkward with Vin and Blair, but he has her thrown over his shoulder, carrying her out of our room and toward theirs.

Mar yells from the en suite, "Come on, boys, aftercare in the big tub!"

"To say this house was a fuck palace last night is an understatement…" Blair has a sparkle in her eyes that I haven't seen from her yet, and I have a feeling it's all the uninterrupted villa time with Vin.

[1]"Yeah, my pussy is quite sore today. And I know the guy's holes are just as bad." I chuckle, and she doesn't even bat an eye at that. Which reminds me, "What the hell is going on with you two and Noah?!"

The smile that spreads across her face says it all. "That's a long story where all of it starts from, but somehow we ended up fucking with him on some camera he had access to… He likes to be in control, so he told us what to do while watching, and it was the hottest thing I'd ever been a part of. Well, that is until yesterday. That was a whole different level." She tips her head back like she's replaying it all in her mind, and I can't deny it was hot as shit. "I might need to get some masks to play with too…"

---

1. Recognize (feat. Drake) - PARTYNEXTDOOR, Drake

Now I'm the one smiling at her, joking, "I love unlocking mask kinks for people."

"Okay, enough about me and my sex life! It's your fucking wedding day, bitch! Let's get to doing your hair and makeup!"

"Fine, but don't think we're not circling back to this conversation. I need the nasty details and all future ones. Two dicks at once is the best thing you'll ever experience," I inform her as we get up from outside the master bedroom where we are having our morning coffee. We're three hours behind Vegas time, so we can get up at our normal time and still be able to catch the sunrise. It's truly breathtaking, and I refuse to miss one morning of it while we're here.

We're walking through the bungalow to Blair's bathroom, where she has the whole thing set up to do god knows what to me. We're keeping things basic for my hair and makeup because my dress is the true show-stopper. Blair went with me right after the guys proposed to pick out my dress. I didn't know what kind of wedding we would end up having, but I sure as fuck was going to have the dress I wanted no matter where it was.

I went with an A-line, sweetheart neckline, and a corset that does magic for my tits. It has off-the-shoulder straps; of course, I had to go with the blush pink. I would rather be shot in the puss than be caught dead in a white wedding dress. The bottom is practically see-through and scandalous enough to keep me entertained for the wedding. The guys aren't going to be able to keep their eyes or hands off of me, and I can't wait to see how good they look in their outfits in front of that icy-blue water as the perfect background.

My only real demand for this wedding was my request that Mack find a good photographer. People always splurge on the dumbest shit when it comes to weddings… but the one thing I will spend a stupid amount of money on is a photographer. We'll have those pictures for the rest of our lives.

Mack comes barging into Blair's bathroom, tattling, "Percy's trying to get me hard! I told him not to because you weren't here, and I don't have my cock cage on… and he won't stop touching me and looking at me like he wants to eat me ali—"

I hold my hand up, cutting him off. "Just because you were such a good boy and came in here to tell me… you two can go have fun."

He narrows his eyes at me. "Is this a trap?"

"No, *Luchik*. We're all about to be committed to one another forever. Go have fun with your *boyfriend* for the last time. That'll be your husband after this evening." He bends down, pressing a kiss on my forehead, and practically runs out of the bathroom, screaming "I love you" over his shoulder.

* * *

Blair's tying up my corset to my wedding dress and won't stop giving compliments. "Mar, you seriously look so good!"

"Thank you, babes, but so do you. Vin's really not going to be able to keep his hands to himself tonight." She blushes at that, probably remembering all the shit they did in front of us, but I'm not letting her forget she watched us do even wilder shit. "Quit blushing, Blair. We did wild shit last night too."

"I know, but I should've asked all of you before if it was okay or not. Vin's so used to it from the club, but what if I made Percy and Mack uncomfortable?" She's nervously picking the skin around her nails, so I grab both her hands.

I look her in the eyes to make sure she's hearing what I'm saying. "If any of us were uncomfortable or didn't want something to happen, we would've stopped right then and there. I promise it doesn't make anything weird." She nods her head, and I keep going, needing to add some humor to cut this serious shit out, "But I am shocked at how well you can ride cock."

She playfully hits my arm. "Stop it!" She pauses, thinks for a minute, and then asks, "Do you really think so?"

Blair and I are walking up to the resort's center where they hold all the events. To say we're turning heads is an understatement. Blair has her sage-green silky dress on that she keeps denying is a bridesmaid dress. The low open back is connected to two thin strings at the front of the dress. She looks gorgeous, and she's carrying herself so confidently now. I have my full get-up on, ready to go see my men when I walk through those doors out to the beach.

Mack has rented out the whole damn place for the five of us, and I think he may have invited the pilot and flight attendants. There is way too much room for just us, but I gave in when we were able to make this our "wedding" instead of the big fiasco he'd been trying to set up back home.

There's an employee by the door waiting to lead us out to the beach. They inform us, "I've got strict instructions not to let you through the door until she's out there, and we get the okay."

[2] "Okay, I'm heading out there. You look beautiful, and I know your guys can't wait to lay their eyes on you… If you see me sobbing, ignore me." Blair pops a kiss on my cheek, turns around, and walks through the doors. I can see Vin and the guys at the end of the walkway; Vin looks a little misty-eyed, and nothing chips away at my frozen heart more than finally witnessing those two getting to be happy together.

My eyes dart to Percy first. He has the forest green suit on with the plain white dress shirt underneath. Nothing out of the norm, but goddamn do those thighs of his fill out those pants better than I've ever seen in my life. Mack has the matching pants, but they're black, and his upper half is what's catching my eyes. He's missing the suit jacket and wears only his shirt. It's an all-white lace that's thin enough that the tattoos covering every inch of his skin peak through the lace design.

Fuck they both look edible.

It makes me giddy that Mack didn't stick to the norm, but what about any of this or us screams normal?

---

2. Another Life - Motionless In White

Mar walks through the doors and is practically floating down the makeshift aisle of sand. I can't do anything except stare in awe. Hot tears stream down my face before I can even register that I'm crying.

[1]Across from me, I look at Percy, and tears are falling down his cheeks, too. It sends me spiraling into full-on, ugly hiccup crying. I see Mar speed up her steps, and finally making it within arms reach, she grabs my face as I peer down at her through my tears. She places a kiss on each of my cheeks, collecting the tears on her lips, then places a gentle kiss on mine, murmuring to me, "I love you, Mack." Then she moves over to grab Percy's face in her hands, going through the same motions, ensuring him, "I love you too, Percy, so much."

The officiant clears her throat, and Mar pulls away from Percy, apologizing to the gal. Clearly, this isn't the ceremony she's used to performing.

---

1. Take Me to Church - Hozier

I've been hearing the photographers snapping pictures as we waited and as Mar was walking down to us.

As I shift on my feet, the oversized plug that's keeping Percy's cum in me—stretched just to his liking—shifts onto my prostate. I suck in a breath which catches his attention, and the immediate fire in his eyes is indescribable. Mar is in the middle, facing the officiant, and looks between us, lifting her brows, wondering what the hell is going on.

She'll find out soon enough.

All three of us are holding hands in a circle, looking like we're about to summon some demons… we probably are, knowing Mar and her hostility toward organized religion.

The officiant starts to go through the beginning of the ceremony, and I zone out, taking in the view of Mar in all her glory. Her dress is breathtaking. It's see-through lace at the bottom and the corset covering her stomach. We match, and we couldn't have planned this better if we wanted to. Her dress is blush pink, while my top is pure white. I'm practically giggling to myself.

Call me a blushing virgin, and your good boy while you're at it.

"Mack, do you have your vows?" I nod to the officiant as she pulls me out of my daydream.

My folded-up paper is in my hand, and I go through my little note of talking points. "I can talk about you two and the love I have coursing through my body all day long, but I'd rather be in that bungalow, on my k—"

Percy cuts me off, "Baby Boy, not right now…" His brows are raised, and I know he means business.

I chuckle, continuing with a smirk on my lips at the growing tent in his pants. "It was you and me, Percy. Before anything, we were best friends, and you quickly turned into someone I couldn't stop thinking about… you made the first move, and after that, I gave in to every desire I kept locked away. I was trying to protect my own heart, but I handed it right over to you, and you've held it for safekeeping. I love you in every inch of this heart of mine, and I can't imagine this life without you beside me." I smile, and he grabs the back of my neck, slamming his lips to mine. "Mar. I didn't see you coming… Actually, I did, but I didn't think it would be so addictive." I smirk at her, and that has her biting her lip, holding back a laugh. "In all seriousness, you came barreling into our lives, and we never want to let you go. You complete us for too many reasons to name off, and I'm so thankful I sent that random message. I love you. If Percy has my heart, you, Marfa Sovereign, own my soul."

I reach up and wipe the stray tear that escaped her eye. "Percy, if you have your vows, go ahead," the officiant says.

[2]"Mack. My Baby Boy. My world. You opened my heart to a side of me I didn't know existed… and I will forever be indebted to you for that. I couldn't imagine where I would be now if our paths hadn't crossed." I think about that for a minute, and I know for a fact he would've been married to some random, bitchy woman with a house in a HOA neighborhood, hating his life…

Thank fuck he did meet me.

He continues, "You brought me out of every shell I ever tried to stay hunkered away in. You make me a better human, a better lover, and a better partner, and for that, I will always be thankful. I love you, Mack, and you always have my heart in your hands."

"Marfa Sovereign. You came crashing into our lives in the best way possible. Any shell I thought Mack had pulled me out of, you cracked open and destroyed. Ensuring I could never turn back, even if I wanted to at times. Your

---

2. ur special to me - Artemas

love for us is fierce and strong, and you've taught me how to unashamedly love both of you, at the same time. Getting to witness you be the badass woman you are in every facet of our lives is indescribable, and I'm thankful just for being able to breathe the same air as you. I love you, Mar. In this life, and every other one my soul gets brought into." Percy moves to kiss Mar. He grabs her neck at the base of her skull, and the kiss pours everything else he didn't put in those vows into her.

I love them both so goddamn much.

Now it's Mar's turn. We all slowly turn to the officiant, and she's wiping a stray tear from her face too. I smile at that, glad that others can witness our love for one another. Blair and Vin have been on each side of the officiant the whole time. Blair's been incoherently sobbing in the background, murmuring how fucking cute we were, and Vin looks like he's about to cut everyone's necks open if he doesn't get to comfort Blair. I nod my head to him, and he gets the hint. He's at her side, rubbing her back, whispering in her ear.

They are precious together.

Mar clears her throat and brings her captivating brown eyes to mine. [3] "*Luchik,* your aura had me pulled in from the moment I met you. You have the kindest, gentlest soul that somehow always brings light to any situation we find ourselves in. You are the light my dark soul needed to meet, and thank you for seeing that darkness and not sprinting the other way. Mack, I love you. To the sun and back."

"To the sun and back," I repeat to her in a hiccup, smashing my lips to hers one more time.

She pulls away from me and spins on her heel to my

---

3. sun to me - mgk

big man. "Percy. Percy. Percy... I was worried about you. I didn't think we would mesh, being so much alike, but somehow we have meshed better than I ever could've imagined, and if I do say so myself, I believe it made both of us better humans. You have a heart of gold, *Papochka,* but you had that golden heart locked up like Fort Knox." She smiles up at him, continuing, "Good thing I knew the code to that safe, and maybe a few guards that helped me break in." She chuckles at that and shoots me a wink. "Percy, I love you and that heart of yours that's in Mack's hands."

He grabs her, picking her up, and she wraps her legs around his waist. He whispers to her softly, "It's in your hands too now, Sovereign."

"Well, I would say kiss the bride, but you all have done what you needed and said what you wanted to say. I now pronounce you husband, husband, and wife?" the officiant says, still confused about why we asked her to pronounce us, but I've always wanted to hear that since I was a little boy.

We all throw our interconnected hands into the air, and as we start to walk back down the aisle, Blair announces, like we planned, "Now, introducing the Sovereigns." Mar looks up at both of us while we're still walking, and I can see the tears lining her eyes. "Fuck... I love you two way too much."

Once we're all at the door, Percy adds a kiss to both of our lips and whispers, "We may not be able to legally be a throuple, but in my eyes, we'll always be the only things one another needs. We both are taking your last name, Mama."

We're walking down the boardwalk to our bungalow after finishing our way-too-intimate dinner that Mack had set up. It included cutting the cake and somehow ended up turning into a goddamn food fight. I chuckle to myself, thinking about Blair yelling at all of us and making everyone stay to clean the frosting off the floor. Something about being in the service industry and people not respecting businesses. We all mocked her, saying, "Okay, Mom," and rolling our eyes. But we did, in fact, clean it all up after the fun was over.

[1] We head straight through the bungalow to the outdoor, over-the-water deck attached to our room. Mar wants all three of us to jump into the water and do the "ruin the dress" trend. The photographers are right on our heels to capture the moment. Blair and Vin split off at the front door, heading up the steps to their section of the house.

One of the photographers is set up by the sliding door,

---

1. hell of a good time - Haiden Henderson

and the other is off to the side to get us from every angle. We only get one chance at this.

Mar is in the middle, and Mack and I are on both of her sides, holding her hands, looking ready to take on the world. I turn to look at Mar, asking her, "You ready, Mama?"

"Yes, *Papochka*," she replies with an appreciative smile.

We both turn our heads to peek over at Mack, questioning him, "What about you, Baby Boy?"

"Ready when you are, *Daddy*." He shoots me a wink after dragging out his favorite pet name for me. I can feel the heat creeping up my neck from the photographers overhearing his antics.

I definitely have a shit ton more courage when I have my mask on.

Mar starts to yell after peeking back and nodding to both photographers, "Ready! Three, two, one! Go!"

We all go running and jump once we reach the end of the deck, throwing our connected hands into the air and kicking our feet up to our butts. Swimming up to breach the surface, seeing Mack and Mar smiling back at me, has me questioning every higher power as to what I did in a past life to deserve these two. I hear the photographers still snapping pictures, and in unison, we all look up at both of their cameras. I'm sure they're getting a hell of a shot of us in this beautiful water.

Mar's dress is floating on top of the water, and Mack's lace shirt is sticking to him like a second skin. Before I can get it out, Mar announces, "Thank you both so much for getting all the pictures of today. If you could see yourselves out... we have post-wedding plans, if you know what I mean." She gives them a tight-lipped smile, and I hear Vin at the door, ready to lead them out of the bungalow. Always looking out for everyone's safety.

Mack breaks the silence, "Am I allowed to be in the

water with this big plug in my ass?" I look at Mar, and she's staring back, kind of wide-eyed, but trying to hide the concern from Mack.

"You'll be fine, Baby, but that does give me an idea… Take those pants off, and climb that ladder with that plugged hole on display for us." My cock has been at half-mast since filling him up and plugging my cum in his ass earlier today.

Mack has his pants flung over his shoulder, ass out on full display as he takes the first steps out of the water, and I all but groan. "That whorish hole of yours looks ready for some cock, Baby Boy." He waves his ass back and forth at Mar and I, both swim to the ladder and climb up as fast as we can to get to him.

Mar is above me, and I can see she decided that no underwear was the perfect idea for our wedding day. Truthfully, I prefer nothing else. Once I get up on the deck, I can see Mar turn her back to Mack, already starting her commands for him, "Be a Good Boy and untie me so I can get out of this thing." He slowly pulls the bow that keeps her corset tight and pulls it through each loop. Mack's cock is at attention, stabbing Mar in the ass cheek anytime he pulls the string through one of the loops.

I run into the room, grab the lube, a couple of toys for Mar, and anything else we might need, and bring it out to the deck. I'm ready to use this gorgeous outdoor space and really put on a show for anyone who wants to listen.

[2]I come back through the door and hear Mar barking out more commands, "On your hands and knees, crawl to me like the Good Boy you are." My knees are about to hit the ground, when she adds, "Come and join me, Percy. We

____

2. Never Lose Me (feat. SZA, Cardi B) - Flo Milli, SZA, Cardi B

can watch our pretty whore crawl to us." She's patting the wooden chaise beside the one she's sitting on.

Mar sits stark naked, matching Mack; I stripped my soaking suit off in the room and threw it in the en suite on the tiles. We're all bare to the world, and I openly appreciate both of them while strolling over to the chair, sitting, and getting comfortable.

I watch as Mack gets to his knees, not breaking eye contact with Mar, and it all feels incredibly erotic. Both of his hands are on the deck.

Mar's practically purring, "Slow, *Luchik*. Nice and slow. I want to see every muscle bunch on those meaty arms and that big cock swaying."

My attention doesn't waver from in between his thighs, but then I remember the plug that I know is still holding my cum, so I instruct him, "Stay on all fours, Baby Boy, you look so pretty like that, but I want to see that plugged hole of yours… turn around for us."

He listens perfectly, spinning around on his hands and knees, putting on a show for Mar and I. He's eating it up, taking instructions from both of us. "Go pull that plug free, *Papochka*. I want to see if he's kept your cum nice and warm for you."

I'm practically tripping over my feet to get to Mack. As my body makes it into his line of sight, he drops the upper half of his body, giving me free rein, and Mar an even better view.

Mar groans, tipping her head back on the chaise. "Satan, Ma'am, thank you for taking your time with these two."

I've decided I'm going to watch these two for a while… maybe even all night. I can get off just as easily watching, but what better way to ring in our commitment than milking both of them bone dry?

Nothing.

Percy has the bottle of lube in one hand and his other is gripping the black plug that's been keeping Mack stretched all day. He starts to fuck him with the plug, pulling it in and out, causing Mack to groan in appreciation. Percy questions Mack, "This hole didn't get enough of me earlier today, did it?"

"No, it didn't, Daddy. It needs more of you. I'll do anything… please just use me," Mack's begging him so pretty already.

Percy looks back at me in question, and I raise my brows. He knows he has to ask and use his words. "Can I fuck our husband, Mama?"

[1]"Yes, and make it good. Your wife wants to come

---

1. ESCORT - Chase Atalntic

while watching; then Mack's going to fill me with his cum," I answer back while grabbing one of my favorite toys to use solo. It's a thrusting dildo with additional suction feature for my clit. That little thing will have me on another planet in under a minute.

Add in watching my hot as fuck husbands together… I'm a goner.

Percy finally pulls the plug from Mack's ass, still positioned up in the air and now begging to be filled. Percy throws the plug on the deck and pulls Mack's cheeks apart. I murmur to them, "Mmm, look at that hole leaking your cum. You better get that cock in there, *Papochka.*"

Percy bends at the knees to use his heavy, lubed-up cock to tease Mack. "Be a good whore and hold your hole open for me," Percy growls.

Mack whimpers as he reaches back, in turn putting all his weight on his shoulder and his face. Once Mack's hands are in place, Percy pulls back, spits on his ass, and then shoves into the hilt.

Why is spitting so fucking hot?!

I question him, "Percy, are you claiming our husband with your spit? We know it wasn't for lubrication…"

Between grunts, he responds, "He's. Ours. This slutty hole is plenty wet enough without the spit." He starts pounding into him at a punishing speed, humming in appreciation. "My little fucktoy loves being used for my pleasure." He's chasing his orgasm with reckless abandon. "I'm going to fill you up and plug it back up so my cum can stay right where it belongs—again."

I flip my toy on, lube up the end that goes in me, and start to work the vibrating cock inside myself. Once the suction hits my clit, I've never been happier that this toy thrusts on its own. I can't see the guys' faces, but the view I have is already too much; being able to see their faces and the eye contact would be more erotic than I can handle right now. Instead, I get to stare at Percy's gorgeous back, broad shoulders, and thighs that I truly wish he would use to crush my skull between, most days. And his ass… His ass needs to be added as an eighth wonder of the world.

Before I know it, he's yelling out that he's coming, and because my body is so connected to both of theirs, I'm pulling the toy away as I come harder than I may have ever come before. Percy's walking back to a still bent over Mack, placing the new, and bigger, plug in his ass that he brought outside with him earlier. Once it's seated in Mack, Percy gives him a parting smack on the ass, causing him to suck in a breath. Then Mack spins around on his hands and knees, crawling without being told. And Percy's smug ass just stands behind him, arms crossed, appreciating the view.

[2]My legs are still sprawled out over the sides of the chaise, and I see Mack start to crawl up the bottom, coming straight for my cunt. "Mmm, I've missed this pussy today, Sovereign." He doesn't even give me time to answer. He dives, mouth first, on my already sensitive pussy.

Percy sits beside me again, hands above his head, fully relaxed and pleased, watching the two of us. "You like watching the whore eat this pussy, Daddy?" The groan that leaves him whenever I call him "Daddy" is worth any cringe I feel.

It's grown on me, honestly.

"He's learned so well, hasn't he?" I give him a hum as an answer.

I'm already so sensitive from coming once, but Mack already has me teetering on the edge of another orgasm.

---

2. Type Shit - Future, Metro Boomin', Travis Scott, Playboi Carti

And all it takes is another hard suck from his talented mouth.

I pull the top of his hair, keeping him right where I need him to be, while coaching him, "Suck, *Luchik*! Fuck, I'm coming! Yes, yes, yes!" I'm using his face for everything I need.

He doesn't give me a second before he's throwing my legs up to my chest and shoving his cock in me like he truly is in charge right now. I'll let him play. It's been way too long since I've been fucked like this.

"I need to fill this greedy cunt up," he grunts between his deep thrusts.

Both of my hands are holding onto the back of Mack's neck. While we're both staring into one another's eyes, he whispers, "I love you so much, Mar."

"I love you, Mack… Sovereign. To a sick extent," I reply, pulling an appreciative smile at my lips. He starts hammering into me, and I feel Percy's hand snake through my leg and slide down my stomach finding my clit with practiced ease. I feel his fingers encase Mack's cock grabbing up some of my wetness and landing on my clit again.

"Are you going to be a good wife and come for both of us, Sovereign?" I have never wanted to be a wife, but fuck does it sound good coming off of their lips.

I grip onto Mack's neck harder, and practically beg, "Harder, Mack. Fuck me like you hate me!" And he does just that.

I'm coming and pulling him down with me. I feel his cock pulsing deep inside me. He slowly pulls out, settling back on his heels in a blissed-out state, just barely managing to murmur to Percy, "Daddy, look at our wife's cum-filled little cunt."

Percy leans over the top of me, taking a look for himself. He smacks my soaking pussy one good time, then growls, "This is my fat, swollen cunt. It's holding our husband's cum so well." He proceeds to lick down my entire seam and shoves his tongue into my hole. Once he's finished to his liking, he pulls back and shrugs. "Had to clean up the mess he made."

I hear one half-assed knock before I see a pissed-off Marcello barging through my office door. "Mar, who's going to fill me in on this issue?" He has his phone gripped way too tightly in his hand, shoving the screen in my face. I'm staring at a picture from our commitment ceremony. A smile immediately pulls at my lips—fuck we all look so happy.

"I don't see an issue you're speaking of, Marcello. Everyone looks happy and in love." I act as dumb as possible because I sure as fuck know what he's enraged about. It's been two weeks since we've been back in Vegas, and that week of peace and quiet seems like decades ago. It's been one problem after another since getting back, so why the hell wouldn't Marcello goddamn Barone be in my office bitching.

"Why does my enforcer—and best friend, I might add —look like he's eating my niece's face off her skull?" They kissed right after we were all announced with my last name. Blair was incoherently crying, so of course, Vin swooped in to comfort her. It all just happened to be caught on camera.

"This isn't my story to tell, Marcello… but I will tell you I've never seen Blair so happy in all my years of knowing her. Please don't ruin this for her… or Vincent, for that matter." I firmly believe that everyone deserves to be happy, whether with or without a partner—or multiple.

"Fuck!" He slams his hand on my desk.

[1]"Marcello, if you want to throw a tantrum, go do that with Ellie and the guys. I highly doubt she puts up with this behavior, either. I sure as fuck don't deal with grown toddlers. My two are at home icing their balls for a reason." His brows pull together in question, probably thinking I knocked their nuts together or something. "They got vasectomies for wedding gifts. You know, since our rights are getting stripped from us daily as women," I say with an unhinged, beaming smile on my face.

None of us wanted kids anytime soon, and I'm more than okay not having to go through pregnancy and birth— if I were to survive. I'm three times more likely to die during childbirth, purely because of the melanin in my skin. They try to blame it on complications, but it boils down to deep-rooted racism and discrimination that runs through the U.S. healthcare system. We can always adopt if we ever want children. I really don't want to stress about traumatizing another soul and bringing it into the danger and chaos that the mafia life brings.

I stand quickly and pack up my stuff, slinging my cross-body over my shoulder, silently telling Marcello it's time to go as we walk to my office door.

"I guess Vin is one of the best options for Blair," he wonders out loud.

---

1. AMERICAN HORROR SHOW - Snow Wife

"Blair's grown, Marcello. I hate to be the one to tell you this, but you don't have a say over who she fucks and who she doesn't. The only one you have a say over is Vin as your enforcer… but I would think about that. He's been loyal to you forever." I give him time to let that sink in, while he's narrowing his eyes at me. I pat his chest. "Okay, I've got to go and check on my man-children at home. You'd think two little half-inch cuts above their sacks wouldn't have them down, but fuck are they milking it," I complain to Marcello as I lock up my office, and we walk out to the parking lot. "And thanks for the plane for the honeymoon, especially so last minute."

"No problem, and thank you for talking me off the ledge, Mar."

* * *

[2] "Here. Now I'm going to smoke and relax." I tell Mack and Percy as I readjust their fresh bags of frozen peas. "Actually, I'm bringing the blunt out here. You two need to chill the fuck out, too."

I head to our spare room, where I keep all my weed goodies, and pull a pre-rolled blunt from its tube.

"It's an Indica. Hopefully it knocks you two out so you can get some rest." Sending a chant down to the devil, I silently ask for a few minutes of bliss. Or at least a few minutes without them bitching about their balls hurting. They wouldn't take the pain meds the doctor prescribed… very strong pain meds, I might add. For one of the most minor surgeries you can get. Women are forced to get an IUD placed with nothing, and they get something to relax

---

2. Adaptation - The Weeknd

them before even stepping foot into the office. Why in the hell we don't at least get that, I'll never know.

We all pass the blunt around a couple of times while sitting on the couch with the low beat of the playlist going in the background. Mack asks both of us, "Can you believe this is where it all started a little over a year ago?"

Percy shakes his head, seemingly daydreaming, and I answer Mack, "Our souls were brought to each other for this exact reason. Somebody, somewhere, knew that we all needed each other in this lifetime."

And I hate to tell whoever's in charge… but these two will be forever Masked & Mine.

ACKNOWLEDGMENTS

Well, there's my debut book. I want to thank every last one of you for reading Masked & Mine! This new version also includes what used to be Forever Masked & Mine and has been re-edited since its first release. The more stories I've written, the more my writing has grown, so I felt Masked & Mine needed a little care post-publication.

A review is so appreciated for a small indie author like me. Now, to the people who made this book possible.

My husband. Mr. Ridge. You probably won't see this, but none of this would be possible if you didn't support every wild idea I come up with. He's the real MVP for testing and making sure the positions in here were even possible. I love you beyond words!

My Beta readers! Abbey, Bri, Olivia, Sadie, and Sierra! You all are beyond amazing! Thank you for taking the risk of beta-reading my debut novel. All your feedback made this book what it is now!

My ARC readers, thank you all from the bottom of my heart for seeing me, a debut indie author, and saying yes! I'm so grateful to all of you!

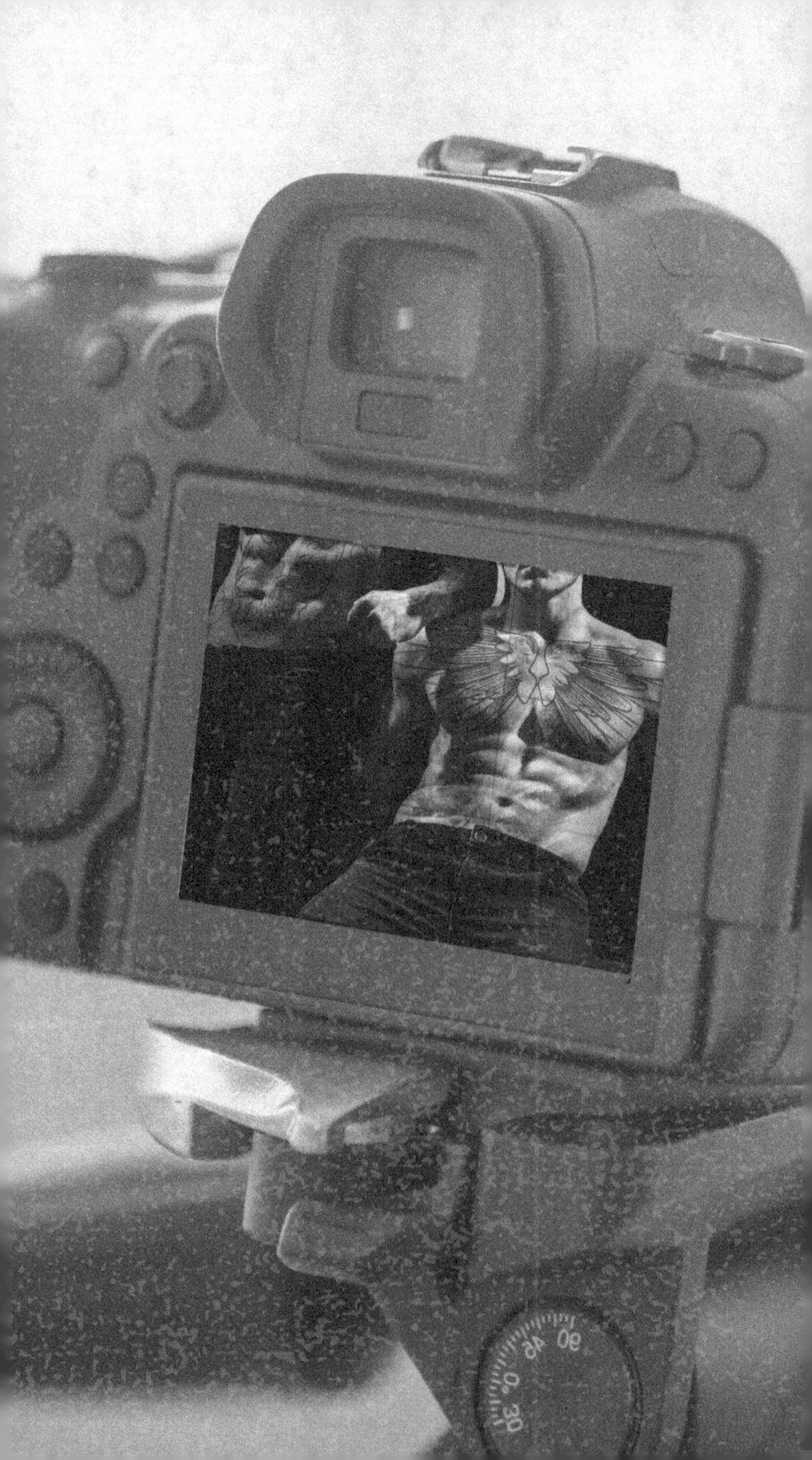

ABOUT THE AUTHOR

Tilly Ridge is a romance author who resides in the middle of nowhere, Kentucky, with her husband, two kiddos, and two dogs. She loves to dabble in a variety of romance topics, themes, and subgenres, but you'll typically find her writing in the dark and polyamory sections of the shelves. Tilly can be easily identified by the pink slush clutched in one hand while her laptop is in the other, ready to write whenever the mood—or the character—strikes! In her free time, she enjoys playing sand volleyball in her local rec league. But what she finds most exciting is her podcast, Releasing Romance, where she shares her knowledge and experience about indie publishing, often bringing on guests to discuss the ins and outs of indie publishing from different professional points of view! This podcast is a passion project of Tilly's as she finds true joy in helping and educating others in a way that is easy to understand.

Join Tilly's readers group for exclusive BTS, art drops, first looks at pretty much anything, and even chapter-by-chapter releases of her ongoing projects at: Tilly's Thots

The newsletter is where the fun is, and maybe even a free ebook will hit your inbox after—along with a first look at the big news.

Find everything you'll need to stay connected at https://www.tillyridgeauthor.com/links

ALSO BY TILLY RIDGE

All future projects will be found here and uploaded as I finish the chapters. Character art prints, early access to news, signed copies sent on release months, a permanent spot on Tilly's ARC team, and so much more!

Click here to access my Patreon.

Also, keep an eye out for upcoming audiobooks that will be released on my website for a lot cheaper than the big retailers!

If you want to read Marcello's story, it's the completed duet below.

<u>Playing for the Dark & Taking Over the Dark</u>: A Completed Duet: A Why Choose Mafia Sports Romance

Las Vegas.

The City of Sin.

What happens here, stays here.

There's only one man in charge: Marcello Barone, leader of the Italian mafia. He's ruthless and unhinged. His only weakness? Ellie Dixon.

For the last year she's maintained her calloused attitude toward men, but at the persistent pursuit from two players of the Vegas Rebels, she finds herself welcoming a little fun.

Nash Hayden, quarterback and number one draft pick, isn't used to the fast life. As he begins his new life, he finds his devotion to his father falters as his spirituality evolves, contradicting everything he thought he knew from his Texas upbringing.

Zamir Prifti, a wide receiver with Albanian mafia ties, does everything he can to hide the darkness woven into his soul. What he doesn't know is how far his family is willing to go to get him back.

Will Marcelo's unwillingness to share sever the connection they've formed?

Or will they learn to play together?

Las Vegas

The City of Sin

What happens here, isn't what it seems.

Marcello has finally decided to share his life, his secrets, and his trust, with people he never saw coming. However, that trust is put to the test when Ellie and Nash disappear, and it all points to Zamir.

Will Marcello and Zamir be able to put everything else aside in order to save Ellie and Nash?

Or in the city of lights, will the darkness finally take over?

**A dark why choose romance. This book is only meant for an 18+ audience. Please read the content and trigger warnings on my website.

Play the Game: A Dark Why Choose Romance

Available on Kindle Unlimited!

Available on audio.

Taking candids turned into so much more...

Marriage never looked easy on the outside looking in, but with Simon, life had been better than ever. I found my soulmate in a man who cared for me, loved me feverishly, and protected me against all odds. But regardless of the love we shared for each other, our eyes often roamed to others. Even at night, when we spent time in each other's arms, we mused over the ideas of what it would be like to explore happily again, while remaining committed to each other.

But fear always held us back.

Then *they* entered the picture.

Nyx. Asher. And Rhodes.

Our best friends.

One daring video to my husband later, and I found myself at the mercy of all four of them days later. All under the disguise of their cosplays' personas—the outfits and attitudes that started it all in the first place.

Taking candids turned into so much more...

What if we can't go back to just friends?

Even if it was just supposed to be one night of fun.

Triple Threat: A Reverse Harem Halloween Short Story

Triple Threat is my newsletter freebie! It's skull face painted triplets with one lucky gal, making all her fantasies come to life!

Strong Side: An MM College Sand Volleyball Romance

Read here!

Clayton Aldrich is everything I'm not, and everything I despise. He's rich, never had to work for anything a day in his perfect life, is the pretty boy on campus, and is always doing everything he can to get under my skin. But when we're forced to become partners, I have no choice but to set my predisposed feelings for him aside. However, as the season progresses, two things become abundantly clear. There's more to Clay than meets the eye, and my feelings for him don't appear to be so black and white.

My entire life has been mapped out for me since the day I was born. Major in business, dedicate every moment of spare time to volleyball, win the Olympics, and when the time comes, take over my father's company. And the only part of that plan that didn't make my skin crawl was playing the sport I loved. Rockwell Campos, the infuriatingly cynical man I feel an inexplicable draw toward whenever he's near, thinks he has me all figured out. But, when we unexpectedly become partners our senior year, Rocky shows me there's more to life than sacrificing who you are and who you want to be in order to be part of a family. Sometimes the families we find are stronger than the ones born in blood.

The two of us may share the same goal, but the question remains… is our strong side, strong enough?

Side Out: An MM College Sand Volleyball Romance

Read here!

I knew from the moment I saw him moving into the house down the street. I knew that a man like Jackson Baker was going to be the one to turn my world upside down. I saw it coming a mile away. But what I didn't see coming was finding out he is one of my patients at my brand new job. I know it's wrong. I know it's against the rules. I know it could destroy the white picket fence that's being thrust upon me, and yet... chasing Jackson Baker is a high I can't seem to quit.

Theodore Young. My neighbor. My Athletic Trainer. My every waking thought. My addiction. I should be spending my fifth year at Palm University--my second chance at the perfect senior year-- making memories with friends, being the team captain everyone is counting on, and setting myself up for a career after college, and yet, the only thing I can think about is him. Watching him. Touching him. Kissing him. He's everywhere and nowhere all at once. But it's not enough. Because he's not mine and I know I can't have him. And yet, whenever I look into his eyes I know...

THE GAME HAS ONLY JUST BEGUN.

Hat Trick: An MMF Hockey College Romance

Available on Kindle Unlimited!

They're best friends. Teammates. They're each other's person.

And I'm, well… me. Dominic Foster and Emerson Baker are Palm University's star hockey players. They're in the prime of their life, and I'm in mine. I'm creating a life for myself, one that I'm proud of. And yet, I see it everywhere I look. Love. I see it in my parents, and in my brother and his new husband. A kind of love so loud I find myself wanting it with everything in me, and I refuse to settle for less. Which is why they're my new addiction. Both of them. Together. What started as a casual fling is quickly starting to feel like it could be more. But is it what I need? Is what they have to offer me, what I deserve? Will I even get a chance to decide before one of them blows the whistle on this entire thing?

Liliana Campos is… everything. She's a tornado of chaos and sass, with a fire burning so bright inside of her she could do anything, have anyone she sets her sights on. She snuck up on both of us when we weren't looking. She wasn't part of the plan. And yet, she feels like she was always meant to be here. She has the power to bring both of us to our knees. It's always been the two of us, but now, we have to decide if what the three of us are building together is something we should run from or hold on to. Because if one of us is done, all three of us are done. That's the rule.

The real question is, are rules meant to be broken, or…

Will we get our own **Hat Trick?**

www.ingramcontent.com/pod-product-compliance
Lightning Source LLC
Chambersburg PA
CBHW071409300726

48976CB00006B/2034